SHOT OF SILENCE

JUSTICE AGAIN #3

M A COMLEY

D1534033

JEAMEL PUBLISHING LIMITED

New York Times and USA Today bestselling author M A Comley
Published by Jeamel Publishing limited
Copyright © 2020 M A Comley
Digital Edition, License Notes

ACKNOWLEDGMENTS

Thank you as always to my rock, Jean, I'd be lost without you in my life.

Special thanks as always go to @studioenp for their superb cover design expertise.

My heartfelt thanks go to my wonderful editor Emmy Ellis, my proofreaders Joseph, Barbara and Jacqueline for spotting all the lingering nits.

Thank you also to my amazing ARC group who help to keep me sane during this process.

And finally, thank you to Jo and Sue from my 'readers' group on Facebook, for allowing me to use your names in this book.

To Mary, gone, but never forgotten. I hope you found the peace you were searching for my dear friend.

ALSO BY M A COMLEY

Blind Justice (Novella)

Cruel Justice (Book #1)

Mortal Justice (Novella)

Impeding Justice (Book #2)

Final Justice (Book #3)

Foul Justice (Book #4)

Guaranteed Justice (Book #5)

Ultimate Justice (Book #6)

Virtual Justice (Book #7)

Hostile Justice (Book #8)

Tortured Justice (Book #9)

Rough Justice (Book #10)

Dubious Justice (Book #11)

Calculated Justice (Book #12)

Twisted Justice (Book #13)

Justice at Christmas (Short Story)

Justice at Christmas 2 (novella)

Justice at Christmas 3 (novella)

Prime Justice (Book #14)

Heroic Justice (Book #15)

Shameful Justice (Book #16)

Immoral Justice (Book #17)

Toxic Justice (Book #18)

Overdue Justice (Book #19)

Unfair Justice (a 10,000 word short story)

Irrational Justice (a 10,000 word short story)

Seeking Justice (a 15,000 word novella)

Caring For Justice (a 24,000 word novella)

Savage Justice (a 17,000 word novella Featuring THE UNICORN)

Gone In Seconds (Justice Again series #1)

Ultimate Dilemma (Justice Again series #2)

Shot of Silence (Justice Again #3)

Clever Deception (co-written by Linda S Prather)

Tragic Deception (co-written by Linda S Prather)

Sinful Deception (co-written by Linda S Prather)

Forever Watching You (DI Miranda Carr thriller)

Wrong Place (DI Sally Parker thriller #1)

No Hiding Place (DI Sally Parker thriller #2)

Cold Case (DI Sally Parker thriller#3)

Deadly Encounter (DI Sally Parker thriller #4)

Lost Innocence (DI Sally Parker thriller #5)

Goodbye, My Precious Child (DI Sally Parker #6)

Web of Deceit (DI Sally Parker Novella with Tara Lyons)

The Missing Children (DI Kayli Bright #1)

Killer On The Run (DI Kayli Bright #2)

Hidden Agenda (DI Kayli Bright #3)

Murderous Betrayal (Kayli Bright #4)

Dying Breath (Kayli Bright #5)

Taken (Kayli Bright #6 coming March 2020)

The Hostage Takers (DI Kayli Bright Novella)

No Right to Kill (DI Sara Ramsey #1)

Killer Blow (DI Sara Ramsey #2)

The Dead Can't Speak (DI Sara Ramsey #3)

Deluded (DI Sara Ramsey #4)

The Murder Pact (DI Sara Ramsey #5)

Twisted Revenge (DI Sara Ramsey #6)

The Lies She Told (DI Sara Ramsey #7)

For The Love Of... (DI Sara Ramsey #8)

Run For Your Life (DI Sara Ramsey #9)

Cold Mercy (DI Sara Ramsey #10)

Sign of Evil (DI Sara Ramsey #11)

I Know The Truth (A psychological thriller)

The Caller (co-written with Tara Lyons)

Evil In Disguise – a novel based on True events

Deadly Act (Hero series novella)

Torn Apart (Hero series #1)

End Result (Hero series #2)

In Plain Sight (Hero Series #3)

Double Jeopardy (Hero Series #4)

Criminal Actions (Hero Series #5)

Regrets Mean Nothing (Hero #6)

Sole Intention (Intention series #1)

Grave Intention (Intention series #2)

Devious Intention (Intention #3)

Merry Widow (A Lorne Simpkins short story)

It's A Dog's Life (A Lorne Simpkins short story)

Cozy Mystery Series

Murder at the Wedding

Murder at the Hotel

Murder by the Sea

A Time To Heal (A Sweet Romance)

A Time For Change (A Sweet Romance)

High Spirits

The Temptation series (Romantic Suspense/New Adult Novellas)

Past Temptation

Lost Temptation

Tempting Christa (A billionaire romantic suspense co-authored by Tracie Delaney #1)

Avenging Christa (A billionaire romantic suspense co-authored by Tracie Delaney #2)

PROLOGUE

"*R*un along now, kids, do what your father says, and I'll see you all later." Grace kissed her two children and her husband, Toby, goodbye and raced back to work.

They'd been shopping for Christmas presents for their extended family. The children had broken up for the holidays, and Toby was looking after them for a few days until Zedex closed down for their annual two-week break. She was exhausted and in desperate need of some rest and relaxation; however, she knew that wasn't likely to be on the cards. Not with two children aged eleven and thirteen to keep her on her toes.

Toby was a taxi driver. He'd been doing flexible hours for the last couple of days so he could look after the kids. She had to laugh at the strain already showing in his features when they'd met up for an early lunchtime shopping trip. The children had pleaded with them to go to McDonald's for a burger. She'd declined, told them to carry on and said she wasn't hungry. The second her family dipped out of sight around the next corner, she'd slipped into the baker's up the road from her firm and bought a tuna mayo roll and a coffee that she would indulge in back at her desk.

She smiled as she walked the fifty feet or so back to work, pleased with what they had accomplished in such a short time. All the presents were now bought, all that was left on the agenda in that department was to wrap them. She'd do that the day before Christmas Eve—she was a meticulous planner, organised at work as well as at home, to the extent it drove Toby to distraction.

Grace loved her life—there was nothing *not* to love about it. She had a good husband; so many of her friends were either divorced or in the process of splitting up. Her two children, Jacob and Abby, were turning out to be self-sufficient and eager to help around the house. From what her friends revealed, her kids' keenness really wasn't matched by any of her girlfriends' offspring.

Yes, she had an amazing life and so much to look forward to on the home front, and work was a breeze at present, too. A few months ago, her boss had sounded her out about potentially offering her a slight promotion which would bring in an extra ten grand per year. Toby had rubbed his hands at the thought of maybe doing less hours himself, but she had instantly put a stop to that train of thought.

Her aim was to work hard now, while they were at their peak physically and mentally, and squirrel the money away for the prime of their lives. She and Toby had ambitions to travel the world once the kids were off their hands and had their own exciting lives to lead.

Before that, they had Christmas to look forward to. Her mother was coming to stay on Christmas Eve. It would be their first Christmas without her father who had died of prostate cancer back in April. She was concerned about her mum who had lately become more and more withdrawn. Her mother had even refused the annual Christmas invitation, but the kids had helped in persuading her to change her mind. Things had got so bad that Grace now feared for her mother's health. How many times had she read about couples who had spent the whole of their adult lives together, dying within a few months of each other through a broken heart?

She pushed the morbid thought aside and upped her pace. The doorman saw her coming and waved. Frank was a true gentleman, always had a great rapport with her, everyone did. Everyone got on well with Grace Hunt.

A noise erupted and Grace instantaneously went down. Frank rushed towards her. She spilt her drink and her roll on the pavement and lay there, staring at a blob of grey chewing gum stuck to the kerb inches in front of her face. Her back spasmed in pain. *Oh God, what's happened to me?* Another noise sounded, and her body jolted again. She could no longer fight the excruciating pain, the numbness in her legs and back. Her eyes closed, and she drifted...

~

*H*e took the shot and grinned as she fell to her knees. Good old Frank rushed to her assistance, ever the gent. He refused to let her live, to get the assistance needed to pull through. She was better off dead. The bullet had pierced her back. He'd been aiming for her spinal cord; it would have embedded itself and paralysed her instantly—that had been his intention, to knock her down so she'd never get to her feet again. She deserved this. The others deserved the fate that was awaiting them also.

So why didn't he feel elated? Would he, in the future? Only time would tell. For now, he needed to get out of there, while he still had the chance to make a clean getaway. He packed his appropriately named .338 sniper rifle away, the one he'd obtained on the black market, so it wouldn't be easy to trace. See, he'd thought his plan through thoroughly in order to obtain the success he was craving. Revenge. All this was about revenge at the end of the day. Sweet revenge as he liked to call it. There were many more to come, the likes London had never seen before. No doubt he would go down in history. That brought a smile to his face as he finished packing his rifle away. He cleaned up any debris, not wishing to leave any DNA yet. That would come in the future, when he upped the ante and started toying with the police.

It was all part of his well-thought-out intricate plan. A plan that had taken him over six months to put in place.

The alarm on his stopwatch beeped. He only had a few seconds left to leave his hidey-hole. He packed up the remainder of his belongings and legged it. Down the stairs from the roof of the building opposite

Zedex. Once the police discovered where the shots had come from, this place would be out of bounds to him, if they ever discovered it.

He reached the bottom of the stairs, slipped his peaked cap lower, covering his eyes, and took a quick glance across the road at the dead woman lying on the pavement. Distant sirens wailed, and the traffic drew to a halt as the drivers rubbernecked the gruesome scene.

Another smile stretched his lips apart. Quickening his pace, he took a left at the corner, then a right and crossed the main road to a small car park several streets away. All in the planning…there was no way the cops would be able to track him down, thanks to all those CSI programmes he'd studied for months on Reality TV. He sniggered and wondered how many other criminals, if that's what he was now, watched the informative programmes. Thinking about it, he supposed not that many, because too many criminals were still getting banged up daily.

Not him.

Nope, he had a lot of mayhem to cause first before he led the cops to his door. There again, all that could change with a click of a trigger. To toy with the police or not? That was the question.

What did he have to lose?

Nothing.

1

*K*aty munched on her egg mayo brown roll and washed it down with a gulp of coffee. "Are you ready for what lies ahead of you this week, partner?"

Charlie swallowed the piece of pasty she'd been chewing on and shrugged. "Were you? When you took your sergeant's exam, I mean."

"Yes and no. I thought I was, but when I got in there my brain froze."

Charlie's shoulders crumpled in front of her.

"You'll be fine. I didn't say that to scare you. You go about things differently to the way I did back in the day. You have nothing to fear. You're intelligent, confident, astute and methodical in your thinking. All the key attributes they're looking for, plus..."

Charlie held up her hand and finished the sentence off for her boss, "And I have good genes."

Katy covered her mouth and laughed. "That, too. I bet Lorne's excited, isn't she? I keep meaning to bloody ring her. You know how it is, once you get home from work all you want to do is chill out with your man."

"Lucky you."

"What's up? Don't tell me things are bad between you and Brandon right now?"

"All right then, I won't. Let's just say they could be better."

"What's the problem?" Katy set her roll down and pushed it aside.

"It's just that on the last case, we worked a lot of overtime, and he sulked because I was never around."

"Tell him to grow up. No, sorry, you don't need me slagging him off, stoking the fires."

"You didn't. I told him the same, that's when the problems started. I don't think he's cut out to be a copper's husband."

"Nonsense, of course he is. All you have to do is point out the pros and cons to this job." She could tell Charlie was trying to suppress a snigger. "Something I said?"

"Pros and cons to being a copper. Where the hell do you begin to keep things balanced? From where I'm sitting, the cons far outweigh the pros, more's the pity. Extremely hard getting the positives across to a partner, and before you say that, AJ understands only because he's a former copper..."

"All right, I won't say that then. I know it must be hard for you both. Get the sergeant's exam out of the way, and he'll be chuffed to bits about your promotion."

"You think? I'm unconvinced about that. We'll see how things go for a few weeks, and then..."

"Then what? You're engaged to him, Charlie. My advice would be to have a serious chat, work out in which direction your lives are going. To me, you seem reluctant to continue, am I right?"

"I suppose I'd call myself confused at present. Anyway, enough about me, how's AJ's new business doing?"

"I'll tell you tomorrow, his first paid job is today."

"Oh wow! How exciting. What is it?"

"A kids' party for a twelve-year-old."

"I'll keep everything crossed for all of it to be a huge success. I'm sure it will be. So glad his parents decided to invest in the business."

"We're classing it as a setting-up loan. As soon as AJ has enough funds in the bank, he's going to repay them. They're really not the type to sit back and *not* interfere, so we have that to look forward to, until we can pay them off."

"Good idea. I think I'd do the same if Mum ever got involved in a business I wanted to set up."

"Really? I couldn't imagine Lorne interfering."

"No, I don't think she would. My pride would want the business to be all about me and not who was backing me. Does that sound bad?"

"Not at all. It makes a lot of sense. In our case, we know that AJ's parents will hinder us and try and have their say on how things should be run. The last thing we want is the business, or the funding, should I say, to cause friction between us. I can't say it's been an easy ride up over the years, up until now."

"Tell me to keep my nose out, but can I ask why?"

Katy sighed and swivelled her cup on the desk. "It boils down to them never wanting him to join the Met. He rebelled against their decision, and they punished him for it. Joining the police was beneath them socially. Basically, they're snobs, and that's not me speaking out of turn, it's fact, they'd be the first to admit it."

"I get that. I don't approve of them thinking that way but I get it. All right, if they felt like that about his decision to join the force, how the hell do they feel about him being a stay-at-home dad?"

Katy chuckled. "I think that was their thought process behind giving us the loan. To help AJ succeed in obtaining a better life for him and his family."

"It's a tough one to call, isn't it? Are they in the right or wrong here?"

"I can see it from both sides; however, it's always better to let adults make their own mistakes or screw-ups in this life. It's how we learn and grow as human beings, isn't it?"

The conversation was interrupted by the phone ringing. Katy wiped her mouth on the napkin and answered it. "DI Katy Foster, how can I help?"

"It's Mick on the front desk, ma'am. I've just heard of a shooting in the centre of London. Are you up for this one?"

"Charlie and I are on our way, have the details ready for us." She ended the call and tucked her half-eaten roll back in the bag and shoved it in the top drawer of her desk as she stood. "Are you ready? There's been a shooting."

Charlie downed the remains of her coffee and followed her out of the office.

"Heads-up, guys. We're going out to attend a shooting. No other details as yet. We'll be back soon. In the meantime, finish up the paperwork from the last case and keep your eyes and ears open for any chatter about this one on the lines."

The team acknowledged the request. Katy and Charlie raced down the stairs and paused at the desk sergeant's counter to obtain the information and to sign out a Taser as their trip could be a potentially volatile situation. "My guys are at the scene, doing their best to cordon off the area—not easy, given the location, ma'am."

Katy glanced down at the paper. "Damn, when you said the heart of the city, I didn't think you meant it."

"I'm not one for exaggerating, you should know that by now."

"I do, Mick."

They exited the station and jumped in the car. There was no need to use the satnav, Katy knew the route well enough. They arrived at the scene around twenty-five minutes later, thanks to the traffic wedging them in for at least five minutes halfway through their journey, after a car broke down at the traffic lights, of all places. The poor woman seemed mortified and grew redder the more the other drivers blasted their horns.

Katy slowed down and shouted at the woman, "Hang in there, I've called for assistance. One of our boys should be with you soon. Have you called the breakdown services yet?"

"I have. They can't get here for another hour or so. I'm so sorry, I feel such a fool."

"It's not your fault. Good luck." Katy drove on. "Poor bloody woman. How embarrassing for her. I wonder if she's run out of petrol."

"Possibly. I'd hate that to happen to me, especially on a main stretch like this."

"Yeah, a real bummer. Here we are. Bloody hell, look at the punters around here having a snoop. What's wrong with people?" She spotted the pathologist's van off to the right and several SOCO vehicles. The technicians were hurriedly trying to erect a marquee over the victim, but the fierce wind was hampering their efforts.

Katy and Charlie left the car after tucking it alongside the vans.

"Hi, Patti. Do your guys need further assistance?" Katy asked.

"Sure, if you have any bodies spare. They'll need to get suited and booted, though, before getting near the corpse."

"I can arrange that. Got any spare suits?"

Patti dipped into the back of the van, extracted a handful of paper suits and handed them to Katy. She set off, leaving Charlie behind with Patti, and distributed the suits to a few of the PCs lingering near the cordon.

"Boys, get over there and help the SOCO team with the tent. The quicker that's up, the likelihood of getting rid of this lot will be in our favour."

Each of the officers took a suit and slipped it on. They sprinted to offer their assistance, and within seconds, between the eight men, they had battled the elements to successfully erect the marquee.

Katy exhaled a sigh of relief and returned to find Charlie already sporting the latest in protective fashion. "Do you have a spare one for me?"

Patti tutted and withdrew another one from the van and threw it at Katy.

"We were told it was a shooting. Any ideas on anything further yet?" Katy held on to Charlie's arm for balance and attached her shoe covers over her new ankle boots. "I'm fit, when you are."

Patti collected her silver case from the van, and together, the three of them entered the tent. Once Patti had removed the coat covering the victim, Katy surveyed the body.

"The doorman placed his coat over her," Patti said. "He saw the incident—really shaken up, he is. I've told him you'll be wanting a word with him. He's inside the building, downing half a bottle of whisky, I shouldn't wonder. Poor bloke."

Katy pointed at the victim. "At least he's alive which is more than can be said for her."

"True dat." Patti grinned. She crouched to examine the victim. "Looks like she was coming back from lunch." She thumbed behind her at the baker's bag and cup with its contents spilt on the pavement close to the woman.

"We'll make a detective out of you yet, Patti."

"Sarcastic cow. I know I was stating the obvious, sometimes it's what is required. What do we have here? Ah, yes, looks like two shots to the back. No idea which one was first. If it was this one, she would've probably been paralysed."

"Maybe the shooter felt sorry for her if his aim was bad and decided to finish her off," Katy replied.

"Perhaps, or maybe that was his intention. To shoot her twice, one to disable her, if you like, and the next to kill her. The shots came within seconds of each other, so the doorman said."

"Did the doorman see anything? Could this be a possible drive-by shooting?"

"He didn't see. He heard the gun go off but couldn't make out which direction the shots came from."

"I take it the doorman knows her then," Katy said. She glanced up and down the street and noted how busy it was. Had the killer intentionally targeted the woman, or had he taken a pot shot in the hope he'd hit someone? The second seemed an unlikely scenario even to her mind.

"Yes, apparently she works in this building at Zedex."

"Hmm…was it a pot shot or did the killer intentionally murder her outside her workplace. Interesting. Could the doorman tell you anything else, Patti?"

"No. My advice would be to go easy on him, he's in shock."

"Understandable if he saw the incident happen and felt helpless in trying to assist her. Was it just the two shots or were there more?"

"The doorman seems to think it was only the two."

"Hmm… So both shots hit their intended target. Not seen anything like this before, have we?"

"I dare say I must have over the years. If you're requesting that I summon up such a case off the top of my head, then you'd be out of luck."

Katy smiled at Patti. "I wasn't. Okay, we'll leave you to get on with things here, and I'll organise uniform, get them to question the crowd, see if any of these fine upstanding citizens saw anything or if they've just popped up, you know, gruesome thrill-seekers."

"My bet is they're the latter. The crowd has doubled, if not trebled, in size since we got here."

"Bloody brilliant. Catch up with you in a moment, Patti."

Katy and Charlie left the tent.

"As I stated, we need to see if any of the onlookers can give us anything. Do you want to organise that while I have a word with the doorman?" Katy asked.

"Sure. Want me to take down a statement from anyone or leave that for now?"

"Leave any likely statements, let's concentrate on the facts for now. See what people saw, if anything." Katy scanned the area. It was built-up. High-rise buildings on both sides up and down the busy street.

"What are you thinking?" Charlie probed.

"Honestly? I'm not sure. If the shooting wasn't a drive-by, then where was the bastard hiding?"

Charlie blew out a breath. "Jesus, that's going to be impossible to ascertain, isn't it?"

"Nothing's impossible, although I admit it's going to test us, but what's new? Look how many windows are facing the scene. We need to get the trajectory of the bullets and then see where that leads us."

"Not an easy case to solve either way, without bloody witnesses," Charlie mumbled.

Katy tutted. "I was thinking along the same lines. Let's get cracking. Dig deep, partner."

Charlie headed off towards the crowd while Katy spun around and entered the building thirty feet behind her. Over by the reception desk, she found two people. One was a man in his late fifties to early sixties. His steel-grey hair was messed up, as though he'd been constantly running his hands through it. The other person was a woman in her thirties with shocking pink hair. Bending over to make sure the man was all right, Katy figured the woman was unaware that her miniskirt had ridden up her thighs and the cheeks of her arse were on show. Katy averted her eyes and approached the pair.

She produced her warrant card. "Hi, I'm DI Katy Foster. I take it you're the doorman who witnessed the incident, is that right?"

"Yes. I'm Frank Windsor. Terrible, terrible thing to happen. She was such a nice lady as well. It still hasn't registered with me yet."

The young woman stood upright and straightened her skirt. "I'm Claire. Poor Frank tried to help her but…"

"Please, try not to upset yourselves. Did you see anything?" she asked Claire.

"No. I heard a faint noise but didn't realise what was going on until Frank staggered back in here and shouted at me to call the police. Not sure how I managed to do it, let alone tell the woman on control what was going on. Why would anyone want to do such a dreadful thing, and in broad daylight as well?"

"That's what we intend to find out, Claire. Are you up to telling me what happened, Frank? No pressure, I appreciate how difficult this must be for you, but the sooner we get the information we're after, the sooner we can punish the person responsible for killing your colleague."

"I understand that. My brother used to be in the force, I'm well aware of how these things work."

"That's good to hear. In that case, you'll appreciate the urgency behind me asking these questions at this distressing time."

"I do." He picked up a glass from the floor beside him and downed the amber liquid. "Something to steady my nerves."

"I quite understand. I would like you to run through the events leading up to the shooting, if you wouldn't mind?"

Frank stared up at her and scratched at the stubble decorating his chin in patches. "I saw Grace coming back from lunch and opened the door for her. I came down the steps, thought I'd get some fresh air. My intention was to join her and have a quick natter on the way back. It's part of our routine, you see. She always had a kind word for me. I would never pester anyone, if they didn't want my company, she did. I regarded her as a dear friend, and now…"

"I'm so sorry for your loss. I appreciate how hard this has hit you, it's never easy to witness the passing of a friend."

"Passing? She was killed. She didn't just die, she was bloody murdered, for God's sake," he bit back. "Sorry, I didn't mean to snap. I'm hurting. My heart is breaking because she has a husband and two kids. That's where she was coming back from—she met up with them for a Christmas shopping trip. She just told me she hadn't had time to eat and said she'd bought a coffee and a roll to eat when she got back to her desk. I keep thinking that if she hadn't stopped off for that she would've been tucked up inside the building a good ten minutes before the incident happened. Such a shame. Hindsight and all that."

"Did you see anyone suspicious hanging around, you know, during your morning shift?"

"I've tried to recollect if I had but all I keep thinking about is the shock on her face as she went down. My heart went out to her. I rushed towards her to try to help her, and that's when the second shot went off. I didn't know what to do for the best. I was torn between diving for cover and remaining there to try and help Grace, but her eyes…they were staring at me without seeing me. I knew then that she was dead. I rushed in here and yelled at Claire to call nine-nine-nine. I picked up my coat and went outside again. I know I probably shouldn't have covered her over, but at the time all I wanted to do was shield her from the onlookers. By the time I got back, there was a small crowd gathered around her. What the hell is wrong with people? If Grace was a stranger to me, I'd be buggered if I'd stand around gawping at her. I stayed with her; I knew I shouldn't touch her, otherwise I would have got down beside her and put her head on my lap. To see a friend, go down like that, someone as nice as her, with a bloody family… I can't tell you how much it hurt, still hurts."

"I know. We're going to do all we can to arrest the person who did this."

"I don't know how you're going to do that. I certainly didn't see anyone odd hanging about. Where were they? Look around you. The number of places where they could possibly hide must be in the thousands, mustn't it?"

"True enough. I can give you my assurance, we won't let this drop until we have the culprit sitting in a cell."

He sighed and then let out a shuddering breath. "I hope that's soon. The thought of having someone that dangerous out there who kills innocent women…it's just wrong, isn't it? What is this world coming to when you can't walk down a main street during daylight hours without getting shot?"

"I agree. These types of incidents are a rarity. That's why it's important to do the groundwork thoroughly. To dig deep, to ask all the relative questions from the outset."

"I can't tell you any more than I have already, I wish I could. I want you to find the bastard, and quickly. What if he comes back? What if he attempts to kill me now that I've spoken to you?"

"I doubt that will happen. All I can advise you to do is to remain vigilant at all times."

"I intend to. Bloody hell, I doubt I'll ever walk the streets again, knowing there's someone out there who is capable of killing innocent people."

Katy exhaled a breath. "Until we find out more it's hard to advise you what to do regarding your own safety. I have to ask, I take it you sat with Grace after the incident, until assistance showed up?"

He nodded.

"Did you happen to see anyone walk by, carrying something bulky perhaps?"

"Like a gun? No, I can't say I did, and yes, I sat on the pavement with her until the ambulance and police arrived, then they shooed me back in here. That's when Claire poured me a shot of brandy. Done me the world of good. I was a mess. My hands wouldn't stop shaking. Claire will tell you, won't you, love?"

"He was proper shaken up. I had to give him a drink to calm his nerves. Bloody terrible situation to be confronted with, worse when it happens to a colleague."

14

"Did you know Grace very well?" Katy asked the receptionist.

"Not really. I've only been here six months, but well enough to say good morning to her and to know a little about her family. She was so proud of her kids. Shit! Her husband, he needs to be called. I did ask the woman on control if I should call him, but she advised me not to and to leave that for the officer in charge to sort out. I think he should be told soon. It's been like over an hour now. I'd want to know ASAP if I were in his shoes, wouldn't you?"

Katy smiled. "I agree. I don't suppose you have an address for her, do you?"

"I don't, but I can contact her boss for you, he'll have it in the personnel file."

"If you can arrange that for me while I speak to Frank, that would be brilliant."

Claire waddled off as fast as her belt-sized skirt and four-inch stilettos would allow her to move.

"How are you feeling now, Frank?" Katy dragged a chair across the floor and sat next to him.

"Numb. Still can't believe it. I've never seen a dead body before, you see. It's bloody tough when you regard that person as a friend. Sickening, it is. Downright despicable. It makes no sense to me, that's what's bugging me about this. She walked towards me with a smile on her face, happy with life, she was, and then to have it snuffed out like that, it's shocking. That's what it is, absolutely shocking."

"It is. Any words I have for you will seem insignificant right now."

"I know. Hard to know what to say to someone who witnesses the light disappear in a friend's eyes. I could do nothing to help her. I have this thought running through my head, it's a daft one really…"

"What's that?"

"That she didn't have time to suffer. Yes, I know there was a delay between the shots, but in all honesty, I don't think it would have registered as a long delay…oh God, I don't know what I'm trying to say, everything is muddled in my head. Does it get better?"

Katy placed a hand over his. "I've heard it can take a few days and sleepless nights to deal with such a trauma. Hang in there. No one will think badly of you if you took a few days off to get over the shock."

"You think I'll need it? My legs, look at them, I can't stop them jiggling. Christ knows what would happen if I tried to stand. Trouble is, I'm usually on my feet all day, looking after people as they come in and out of the building. I wouldn't be up to doing that."

"Maybe Claire could suggest that your boss sends you home. Do you have anyone there?"

"No, my missus walked out on me five years ago. Went off with one of those toy boys or whatever they're called. Thirty years younger, can you believe that? How is a man of my age supposed to compete with a youngster? I'm closer to my grave than he is to his nappy era."

"Sorry to hear that. Do you have friends or other family members? Someone who could stay with you a few days?"

"Not really. I'm a loner when I'm not at work. That's why these people mean so much to me. All we might do is share the odd smile, but they treat me well. Friends and family always seem to shaft you these days, that's why I prefer to keep my distance."

"I can understand that, especially after what happened with your wife." Katy glanced up and removed her hand from his as Claire joined them again.

"I've got an address for you." She handed Katy the piece of paper.

"That's very kind. I'll go and break the news to her family and then come back. My partner and I will need to question the staff, see if they have any ideas about what's gone on today."

"I'll let the boss know." Claire returned to her desk again.

"Will you be okay?" Katy couldn't help but be concerned for the man sitting next to her. He still appeared to be in shock.

"I think so. I don't want to hold you up. You should get over to see Toby. Once you've told him, will you send him my regards and an apology for not being able to do more to help Grace?"

"You mustn't think like that, Frank. You're not to blame. You did all you could to help her in her moment of need. I'm sure if she was looking down on us she would be gutted to hear you speaking like that."

He gulped and asked, "You think?"

"I know. I'm going to make tracks now, I think you should do the same. You're not fit to be at work. Do you need a lift?"

"No. I have my car here today. Maybe I'll call for a taxi instead."

"Good idea. Claire, can you call a taxi to pick Frank up?"

"Sure, I'll do it right away."

Katy patted Frank's knee, her heart going out to the man.

"I'm sorry I was useless. Will you need a statement from me?"

"Yes, in a few days. Why don't you contact your brother? You said he used to be in the force, didn't you?"

"He did. He's dying of lung cancer, I'd rather not burden him with this, if it's all the same."

"Damn, sorry to hear that."

"It is what it is. Damn fool smoked over forty fags a day due to the pressure of his job back in the day, and now he's suffering for that assumed enjoyment." He shuddered. "Whoever invented cigarettes should be strung up for killing millions of people over the years. Not right, is it?"

"Don't get me started on that one. I detest smoking. I totally agree with you. Okay, if you're sure you're going to be all right, I'd better go and see Toby. Take care of yourself. I'll be in touch in a few days with regard to taking a statement."

"I look forward to seeing you again. Please, promise me you'll do your best to get this bastard."

"You have my word on that." Katy patted his hand again and rose from her seat. "Stay there until your taxi arrives."

Claire smiled. "I'll make sure he stays put."

Katy smiled and nodded. "We'll return later, if you could let your boss know."

"I'll do that," Claire replied.

*K*aty and Charlie left the car and walked up the long path to the semi-detached house. The garden was looking sorry for itself now that December was here and the cold weather had arrived, but Katy could tell it had been well cared for. Had that been Grace's job? "Are you ready for this?"

"Does it get easier, the more you do?"

"Not really. I was relieved when the task used to fall on your mother's shoulders. I've never relished telling a relative the inevitable." Katy rang the bell and inhaled and exhaled a few steady breaths.

"You'll be fine," Charlie whispered.

The door opened, and a man in his early forties frowned at them. "Hello, can I help?"

Katy and Charlie flashed their IDs, and Katy announced, "DI Katy Foster, and this is my partner, DC Charlie Simpkins. Would you be Toby Hunt?"

"I am. What's this about?" Toby's frown deepened.

"It would be better if we spoke inside, sir."

"Can you give me a clue? How do I know those IDs are real? You hear of so many scammers these days."

"You can check by all means. Ring the station if you wish. Whatever makes you happy."

He relented and stood behind the door. "Come in. You'll have to excuse the mess, leading up to Christmas."

"No problem."

They followed him through the house to a large lounge at the rear.

"Take a seat. Now, why are you here?"

The three of them sat down. A large thump sounded overhead.

Toby raised a finger. "I'm warning you, I'm going to shout. *Kids, pack it in. I have guests.*"

The noise ceased. Katy nodded her appreciation and then said, "I'm sorry to have to tell you your wife was involved in an incident today."

"What sort of incident? I was with her only a short while ago. Is she all right?" His voice rose the more he spoke.

Katy sighed. "I'm sorry, no. Unfortunately, your wife died at the scene."

His neck extended forward, and he blinked continuously as the words sank in. "What? Is this some kind of joke? She can't be dead. I don't believe it. I refuse to believe it. Did she have an accident? What happened? I need to know. Please, don't keep me waiting…how did she…?"

"I know this is hard to hear, Toby. I'm afraid your wife was shot."

He shook his head and launched himself out of his seat. He paced in front of the gas fire and shook his head in disbelief. "I can't believe what I'm hearing. How? We met her less than two hours ago and spent her lunch hour sorting out Christmas presents. No, I don't believe you, she can't be dead, she just can't be."

"Take a seat, Toby."

He flopped into his seat again and stared at Katy. "I'm waiting. What happened? How does someone get shot when guns are illegal?"

"That's what we need to investigate. The doorman was with your wife when she died, if that's any consolation. He's in shock right now."

"Was he hurt? Where did this occur?"

"Outside her place of work. No, Frank wasn't hurt in the incident. He was with her come the end. What I'm trying to say is that she didn't die alone."

He placed his hands against his cheeks. "God, I…I can't take this in. She was so happy. Shot, you say? How?"

"I need to ask you some questions. Do you think you're up to answering them?"

"I don't know. All I can think about is her lying there with a stranger, or the doorman from work by her side instead of me. God, what the hell? How does something like this happen in London? Was it gang related?"

"At the moment, we can't tell you much. We're interviewing possible witnesses but haven't come up with anything substantial as yet."

"Someone shoots a person, that person being my wife, and you don't have a clue who's done it?"

"That's right. Whoever the culprit is we believe he took a risk; he's bound to have made a mistake along the way."

"Why? He successfully killed my wife, that's a big mistake, but I take it that's not what you meant."

"No. Sorry. I need to ask if your wife had any enemies, Toby."

"Enemies? You think someone she's fallen out with would be capable of carrying out such a...a...vile act? I don't know... Shit, my head hurts. Bloody hell, how am I going to tell the children? What with Christmas just being around the corner... Will we ever learn to deal with this...loss? Jesus... What about her mother? She's not in good health after her father died, now I have to tell her that her daughter is dead as well!" He let out a sob and then sucked in a deep breath, trying to keep himself from breaking down.

"So, am I to understand that she hasn't fallen out with anyone recently?"

"No. My wife wasn't the sort. She's...she was friends with anyone and everyone."

"What about in the past? Is there something there that we should know about?"

He paused to ponder the question for a few moments. "Such as what?"

"Anything, anything at all?"

"I can't think of anything. We've been together over fifteen years. Neither of us has any exes to contend with, not really. We dated a few people for a couple of weeks, nothing major in my eyes."

"May I ask what work your wife did?"

"She worked as a stockbroker at Zedex."

"I see. And what about you, Toby?"

"I drive a cab for a living. I'm taking a few days off. Grace was due to break up for the Christmas holidays soon, and then she was going to take care of the kids during the day. Damn, I'm due back to work in a few days, a heavy period ahead of me, how am I supposed to do that now, with no wife here?"

"Can you ask family members to help out? How old are your children?"

"Eleven and thirteen. I suppose I could ask my sister at a push, but she works full-time and has kids of her own to look after."

"I'm sure someone will step up to the plate and help out soon."

"And if they don't? I can't believe I'm thinking about the future, I need to live in the present, I need to know about my wife. Did she suffer?"

"I don't think so. Frank was there, as I said. She was shot once, he rushed to assist her, and then the second shot came a few seconds later. Not enough time in between for her to figure out what had happened to her—that's my take on it after listening to what Frank had to say about the incident."

"That's a relief, though it doesn't excuse the fact that someone would want to do that to her. Are you telling me this was intentional? Why couldn't she have been in the wrong place at the wrong time? Maybe there's a madman on the loose, they have them all the time in the States, don't they?"

"They do. At this moment, it would be remiss of us to rule out any possibilities. Tell me about your relationship. Were you and your wife happy, no marital problems at all?"

"Yes, very happy. We sat down most nights as a family to eat meals, I managed to work that in around my shifts. Popped home if necessary, between jobs, and then went straight back out again. It was important for us to keep up a united front in that way." He paused and shook his head. "She's gone, and I didn't get the chance to tell her a final time how much I loved her. I'll never feel whole again, ever. We were together at lunchtime, all of us, the kids included. Christmas shopping." He pointed at the pile of carrier bags in the corner. "She told me to leave them alone until she got home, that she would see to putting the gifts away."

Tears formed and slipped onto his cheeks. He wiped them away with the back of his hand. "Does it ever get any easier? The pain? I feel numb inside. I know I have to hold things together for the sake of the kids… Oh God, we were due to go out tonight."

"May I ask why? Was it a special occasion?" Katy asked, swallowing down the huge lump in her throat.

"It's our anniversary…fifteen wonderful years we'd been together. Now all that has gone. The flame of our love has flickered and died… I can't imagine what our lives are going to be without her, now that Grace is gone."

"I'm so sorry to hear that. You have my deepest sympathy."

"Thank you, but it won't bring her back, will it?"

Katy sighed. "Sadly not. I can see how upset you are. Would you rather we left our questions for another day?"

"No. I don't think so. I need you to find this person and punish them to the best of your ability. Never let them walk the streets again after robbing me of my beautiful wife. How can such a perfect soul be snuffed out like that? We all have a life expectancy, we're born with that, how do you comprehend losing a loved one at forty-two? Her whole life lay ahead of her. Our plans for the future disintegrating like that, only to remain as distant memories."

"Toby, is there anyone we can call? Ask them to be with you?"

"Only my sister within the area. She'll be at work. I don't want to disturb her. She has her own life to lead, it wouldn't be fair to drag her into this, not yet."

"As you wish. What about a good friend?"

"My wife was my best friend. We rarely mingled with others, what with both of us working full-time and having two children to occupy the rest of our time."

"I understand." Katy was at a loss to know what to say next.

Charlie jumped in with another question to get her out of trouble. "Did your wife mention that she'd felt uncomfortable lately? Perhaps she thought someone was watching her."

He thought the question over for a second or two and shook his head. "No. If that had cropped up, I wouldn't have let her out of my sight. What am I saying? I couldn't be with her twenty-four-seven, we both had separate jobs to do. Are you saying someone might have been following her around and we didn't realise it?"

"Perhaps." Katy replied, grateful for Charlie stepping in. "As I said, at the moment, all we can do is ask the questions, hoping they'll give us some insight into what's gone on in the lead-up to what happened to your wife today. If we can't find anything along those lines then we'll be forced to believe that your wife was obviously in the wrong place at the wrong time and someone took a pot shot or two just for the sake of it."

"Hard to fathom," he whispered. "Disgusting if that turns out to be the truth. What a waste of a life…" His voice trailed off.

"Indeed. If you have nothing for us, we're going to go back to her place of work, see if there's anything there, unless you know of any problems she'd had recently there."

"No, she loved her work. She got on really well with her colleagues. They're very supportive of one another, even though their environment can be fraught at times."

"High pressured, you mean?"

"Yes, the stock market is up and down, as you probably know. Dips and rises, but she never brought any of that angst home with her. She left it at the door. Not sure I would've been able to do that if I was in her position. That shows you the type of character she was. Placid in her home life, eager to make all our lives better and less of a challenge when things went wrong at work. Am I making any sense? It sounded jumbled even to my ears."

"I understand what you're saying, Toby, don't worry. I hate to repeat myself, but do you think you're going to be all right when we leave?"

"Yes, I have a lot to consider. I need to find the right words to break it to the kids. What should I tell them?"

Katy shrugged. "The truth, that their mother won't be coming home again and leave it at that for now."

He stared at her. "My kids are very astute, they won't be satisfied with that statement, Inspector." He waved a hand. "Don't worry, I'll figure it out. You have enough on your plate trying to find a reason, and the killer." He rose from his seat and walked over to the door.

Katy and Charlie followed him back into the hallway.

He shook their hands at the front door. "Promise me you'll do your best for my wife."

"You have my guarantee on that. Sorry for your loss. Here's my card. If you need to speak to me, please reach out, don't bottle things up."

He smiled at that. "Is that a man thing, do you think?"

"Probably. Take care of yourself and your children, Toby. I'll be in touch with any developments soon."

"Thank you. Good luck." He bowed his head and closed the door gently behind them.

"Jesus," Charlie said, heaving out a large breath. "I don't envy him having to tell a couple of teenagers, or thereabouts. What a dreadful situation."

"Yep, life's a bundle of laughs at times and a pile of shit at others. This situation definitely belongs in the latter category. That was tough."

"Too right. And we've gleaned nothing from the visit at all."

"Unfortunately. Let's hope her workmates will be able to point us in the right direction, otherwise it's going to be yet another albatross around our necks."

They got back in the car, and Charlie chuckled.

"Sorry, not appropriate in the circumstances, but you do come out with some strange sayings."

"Glad I amuse you. It makes the day go quicker, right?"

"It does."

2

*T*he young receptionist greeted them with a warm smile the moment they walked into the building.

"Hello again, back so soon?"

"Yes, we need to interview Grace's work colleagues."

"I get that. I've been sitting here trying to think of anything that might have happened over the last week or so and I keep drawing a blank. I wish that wasn't the case. Poor Grace, I can't stop thinking of her, lying on the pavement, her eyes wide open."

"You're going to have to stop punishing yourself like that, otherwise it'll make you ill. Did Frank get off okay?"

"Yep, bless him. He was super cut up about it. He really, really liked her. Used to tell me she was one of his favourites. Never looked down her nose at anyone even though she was a high-flyer upstairs, at least I think she was."

"That's good to hear. Would it be all right if we went up?"

"Sure. I'll ring ahead and let Jake, the security bloke up there, know you're on your way." She pointed to the lift in the corner and picked up the phone. "You want the top floor."

Katy and Charlie waited for the doors to open and then jumped in.

Katy punched in floor six and blew out a breath. "Can't say I'm looking forward to asking the same bloody questions over and over in the hope that someone has a tiny snippet of information we can follow up on."

"I hear you. What else can we do without any other clues to go on?"

"Not a lot. Let's hope Forensics come up trumps with something soon. I have an ominous feeling about this one."

"Shrug it off. It'll only get in the way," Charlie advised.

Katy smiled at her. "That's something your mum would say. How is she?"

"Fine. She asks how you're doing all the time."

"Checking up on me, eh?"

"No, I didn't get that impression. More out of concern. I told her I love working alongside you and that we make a good team."

"Ouch! How did that go down?"

"Fine. She was genuinely pleased. She told me to send you her love and a reminder that you and AJ have an open invitation to visit."

"That's kind of her. She's never far from my mind, you know. You can't work with someone over ten years and stop thinking about them just because they leave. Maybe the three of us will take her up on that invitation soon. I'm sure Georgie would be in her element surrounded by the dogs. She's always asking if she can have one."

"What a sweetheart. You should get her one. I think growing up with animals is a good foundation for kids, as long as they treat them with respect, that is."

Katy puffed out her cheeks. "Impossible, especially now AJ has started his business. There are not enough hours in the day to consider taking on an extra burden at this time."

"Such a shame. I get that. I've always had dogs in my life yet now, I go home and it's just Brandon and me. Something seems to be missing."

"Can you not get another rescue?"

"It wouldn't be fair. Not on the dog to be left at home all day. Dogs are sociable animals. It really pisses me off when people work full-time and complain if their dogs leave them a package at home on the living room carpet. Mum had a friend once, her husband died of cancer, the dog was really his; she was jealous of it, in fact. She was out of the house ten hours a day and hit the dog when she got home and found she'd weed and pooed in the kitchen. She handed the rough collie over to Mum, said she couldn't cope with it any more. Mum got the dog checked over by a vet—she came to us with cystitis. The heartless bitch hadn't even taken her to the vets. Mum struck her off her friends' list after that."

"How sad. What happened to the dog?"

"We found her a loving home with a retired couple. Not long after, we learned she'd died of pyometra because the previous owners hadn't been responsible enough to spay her. She was such a beautiful dog, died way too young, she was only nine."

"Oh God, I'm filling up here. Why are people so irresponsible? Did they breed from her?"

"Not as far as I can remember. Some people just..." The lift pinged, and the doors sprang open. "Saved by the bell. Don't get me started on negligent owners not doing the best for their animals."

"Ha, we're supposed to be a nation of animal lovers, and yet some of the tales we hear about how animals, dogs in particular, are treated could curl your toes. Makes you ashamed to be British at times."

"Yep, just glad places like Mum runs exist. She'd never see a dog on the streets. Back to business."

Katy smiled. "We do get riled up about things. What a pair we are."

"Shows how much we care and the compassion we have running through our veins."

"True enough."

They approached the security guard and showed him their IDs.

"Hello, ladies. I was informed about your imminent arrival. Come this way. I'll show you through to Mr Markham's office. He's been expecting you. Such a dreadful thing, losing Grace. She was a wonderful lady. Always had a kind word to say about everyone."

"Hopefully we'll get to the bottom of why it happened, soon."

"I hope you do. We hear of so many cases not being solved these days…not that I'm blaming you guys. I'm sure you do your best with the funds you have in place."

"Departmental cuts are the bane of our lives, that's for sure. We're extremely proud of our arrest record all the same, if that's any reassurance."

"Congratulations. Here we are, ladies. Can I get you a drink? I'm sure Mr Markham won't mind me asking."

"Coffee, white with one sugar. Thanks, that's very kind of you."

"I'll fetch them in. Go through."

Mr Markham was on the phone. Seated behind his large walnut executive desk, he gestured for them to take a seat and held up two fingers, signifying how long he was likely to be before he could give them his full attention.

The security guard returned and handed Katy and Charlie a paper cup each. "There you are, ladies. Enjoy," he whispered and backed out of the room.

Mr Markham swivelled in his chair and turned to view the London skyline visible through the sizeable picture window and laughed before he ended the call and faced them again. "Sorry about that. I haven't spoken to my chum in a few months. Not an ideal time for a catch-up chat, but some people can never take the hint. I suppose you're here about Grace?"

"That's correct. We needed to shoot off to break the news to her husband before we spoke to anyone here. We're going to need to interview all of her colleagues. Do you have many people working here?"

"A couple of hundred. How did Toby take the news? No, that was probably the dumbest question I've ever asked in my life."

"Yeah, not good. He was about to tell the kids when we left. Ouch, a couple of hundred, you say?"

"Yes, however, I was teasing a little, it's just my way. The people who worked closely with Grace you can count on one hand, I suppose."

"That's a relief. Would it be possible to have a word with them?"

"Of course. Will it take long?"

"I'm not sure. I suppose it depends on what information they can offer us. Let's start with you, shall we?" Katy replied brusquely. The man's attitude sucked in her eyes. Here he was, laughing while, as they spoke, his colleague was probably being cut open at the mortuary by Patti.

"Go on then, what do you want to know?"

"Did Grace ever come into contact with the general public in her role?"

"No. Well, what I mean by that is no, not face to face, only over the phone, occasionally. We tend to deal with the big corporate firms here, very rarely with investors taking a punt on the stock market, although it has been known now and again. You know, if someone has been left a large sum in a family member's Will, an inheritance, or been left a house and they ring up to enquire about the best way to invest their money."

"Really? They come to you as opposed to going to a financial expert?"

"People try to cut out the middleman, see financial advisors as a waste of money. Some can be, but most of them are okay. You'll always get the odd person trying to save money, though. I can see if she's dealt with any members of the public lately, if that's what you want?"

"It would definitely be a help. We'll need a list of people she'd possibly spoken to over the past couple of months, if that's all right?"

His shoulders slumped, and he collapsed back in his chair. "That could take weeks to sort out. We have over...what...? I suppose a hundred thousand or more clients, that's off the top of my head."

"Crikey. I didn't really think it would be that many. Do your best, maybe over the past few weeks rather than months, in that case," Katy corrected. "We'll also need to speak to the colleagues she came into contact with daily also."

"That's easy enough. I've only just promoted her, within the last month or so. She had a team of four under her. I can arrange for you to see them all, organise a spare room to talk privately with them, if that's what you want?"

"That would be excellent, as soon as we've finished talking. What was your take on Grace?"

He shrugged. "She was a very likeable character. She had a stubborn streak, which was what drew me to her and ended up being the main reason I promoted her."

"I see. Stubborn, as in?"

"She knew her own mind and wasn't easily swayed by others. Willing to work on her own initiative without knocking on my door every two hours or so, seeking advice on what to do when certain queries cropped up, like her predecessor did."

"Okay. About her predecessor, was that person male or female?"

"Male. Bill Enright, he was ancient really. Sixty-two. I should have had the balls to get rid of him a few years back."

"May I ask why?" Katy asked as Charlie jotted down the executive's answers.

"Because as soon as I initiated the change, our profit margins leapt up to another level, a much higher level."

"All because of Grace Hunt's efforts?" Katy asked, unsure how the dynamics of her team worked.

"Indirectly, yes. She was open with her team. Told them to come to her when they had problems that needed solving rather than stew on things, which Bill used to encourage during his tenure as leader. The team's confidence appeared to improve overnight. I know most people will find that hard to believe, but it's true. In my opinion, she was one in a million." His head bowed, and he coughed slightly. "I will miss her. One of those people who brightened your life when she said hello to you, if that makes sense? Although there was a more ruthless side to her which bubbled beneath the surface on occasions."

"She sounded an amazing character. A person who could solve any problem fairly perhaps?"

"Oh yes, that times a hundred. I noticed the change in the staff within a day of her taking over. Wait, maybe I'm exaggerating there a touch, let's call it a week. As I said, profits rose at the same time and, let's face it, that's the most important thing in our line of business."

"Great to hear that someone is capable of turning a firm around like that. You'll miss her input around here, I should imagine."

"I will, in more ways than one. I'll have to see what the others have to offer now before I can appoint a replacement. This will knock the stuffing out of them for a while, it's bound to, isn't it?"

"I would think so, yes. Do you usually promote internally? Or do you open up the interviews to outsiders as well?"

"I always do the latter as a matter of principal. There's a chance I could strike it lucky and snap up a super-experienced candidate who has relocated to the area, perhaps. I tend to steer clear of people who have left a rival firm lately. And, before you ask, that's just my suspicious mind at work."

Katy smiled and nodded. "Always good to have some form of doubt guiding you in business."

"Oh yes, especially a financial business. It's seen me right over the years."

"And there were never any ill-feelings with any of Grace's colleagues?"

"No, she got on with everyone. Any conflicts are generally worked out within a few hours of them arising. I believe in running a happy ship. It keeps things stable in choppy waters, and there's been a fair few of them over the past few years. The stock market has been up and down like a prostitute's undies, if you'll excuse the analogy."

Katy grinned. "You're excused. What about jealous partners?"

He frowned and sat forward again. "I'm not with you."

"If you say everyone got on well, is there a possibility that Grace got on too well with one of her colleagues?"

"Never, not Grace, I refuse to believe that of her. She was happily married with kids."

"I should think, over the years, that's been said about a lot of people who have managed to stray with work colleagues. What about Christmas parties, under the mistletoe perhaps?"

He shook his head and tutted. "You couldn't be more wrong. Grace was above all of that. She loved the bones of Toby."

"Okay, that's good to hear. I didn't mean to cause any offence. I had to ask, please forgive me."

"Of course. I understand you have a job to do, but surely, if I've given you a character assessment already, why would you then try to tarnish her name?"

"I wasn't aware I had. All I did was ask a genuine question."

"I'm sorry, maybe I was wrong to snap. My feelings are a tad raw right now, as you can imagine."

"I can. I really didn't mean to offend you. It's just if I don't ask the questions, I won't obtain the answers needed to get the investigation off to a good start."

"I get that. Maybe you could be a little less sharp-tongued with the staff. They're deeply mourning her loss, to the extent that trade is down by half today." He waved his hand. "Not that I'm concerned about that right now, I just wanted to make you aware of the situation and how much they've been affected by this godawful news."

"Duly noted. I'll be careful where I put my size fives, I promise."

"Okay. In that case, do you need me for anything else?"

"No, you're free to go about your day."

He rose from his seat and crossed the room to the door. "I should only be ten minutes. Make yourselves comfortable until I get back."

He closed the door behind him, and Katy heaved out a sigh. "I wasn't heavy-handed, was I?"

Charlie's brow furrowed. "On the contrary, don't go beating yourself up for him misinterpreting something. You asked the obvious questions needed to proceed."

"Thanks for the reassurance, Charlie, I was beginning to doubt myself for a moment there. What do you think?"

"It's hard to say. She was obviously well-liked and enjoyed her job."

"Yeah, we'll see what the others have to say about her character without their boss' ears flapping and go from there. Maybe this was a one-off, pot-luck kind of shooting and not a stalkerish type after all."

"Who knows? Something we should be aware of, I suppose."

Katy took the opportunity to ring the station.

Karen answered her call. "Everything okay, boss?"

"Yes and no. We might as well get the background checks started on the family, if you would, Karen. It's Grace and Toby Hunt."

"On it now. Anything else you want us to look into?"

"CCTV footage of when the shooting occurred on Tybold Street. There are lots of buildings around, some of them are sure to have cameras. That's it for now, Karen."

"Leave it with me. I'll get Graham on the task. He'll ring you if he finds anything."

Katy ended the call, and within seconds, Colin Markham had come back into the room.

"Okay, ladies. I've rearranged the furniture a little in the conference room. Would you like to come with me?"

Katy and Charlie followed him up a narrow corridor. The rooms either side were behind glass, so all the other members of staff looked up as they passed.

The conference room had solid walls but a glass door.

"Will this do you?" Colin enquired.

"It's perfect, thanks so much."

"Not a problem, happy to oblige. Do you want me to send the first one in?"

"If you wouldn't mind. Who will that be?"

He paused to think. "Shall we go by seniority?"

"Makes sense to me," Katy agreed.

"In that case, Steve Abbott will be first. I'll ask him to join you."

Katy and Charlie took a seat and were settled ready for the interviews to begin within moments. Steve Abbott joined them not long after. He was in his mid-to-late forties with black hair tinged with grey at the sides and bright-blue eyes which appeared to be somewhat watery.

"Hi, I'm Steve. The boss said you'd like a word with me."

"Hi, Steve. I'm DI Katy Foster, and this is my partner, DC Charlie Simpkins. Please, take a seat. We promise not to keep you too long."

His smile seemed false, and he pulled out a chair. "How can I help?"

"As you're probably aware by now, Grace Hunt lost her life this morning. We're trying to form a picture of what happened in her daily life that could have possibly led to her murder."

"Murder...I never thought I'd ever hear that word, not personally, not about anyone I knew anyway. Hard to believe she's no longer with us. My heart goes out to Toby and the kids."

"You knew the family well then?"

"Yes, we're a really close-knit unit. We work exceptionally long hours and don't tend to socialise much except with each other. We take it in turns to hold a barbecue at each other's house in the summer. Winters are a different story, of course. I suppose we all tend to hibernate when it's darker evenings. Sorry, I'm waffling. I tend to do that when something doesn't sit right with me."

"Learning a close friend has just been killed can definitely take its toll on people with a sensitive nature."

"I'm not sure if I have one of those. What I will say is that we're all struggling to come to terms with losing her. Never in my wildest dreams would I ever think someone could hate a person enough to want to end their life like that. It's callous, evil and beyond my comprehension. I keep asking one question over and over...why? It doesn't make sense, not one jot."

"It doesn't to us either, hence our need to interview those who were closest to her. Is there anything you can tell us about Grace?"

"No, except vouch for her wonderful character and her willingness to help those around her."

"Do you mean workwise?"

He shook his head.

Katy continued, "Can you give me an example?"

"One of the guys had a lot of expense when his car broke down. Ben, it was, he'll fill you in on the details, I'm sure. Anyway, at the end of the month he found he didn't have enough to pay his rent, and good old Gracie dipped into her savings to help him out. Not sure if her husband, Toby, knew about the loan or not, she didn't seem the type to keep secrets from her husband. Anyway, there are not many folks who would go to such lengths to help out a colleague in need, right?"

"I suppose so. Did Ben pay the loan back?"

He shrugged. "You'll have to ask him."

"We will. Thanks. Regarding her colleagues, had anyone fallen out with her in the past? If so, what was the reason?"

"I don't think that's the case at all. You should see everyone in that room, they're all devastated, and rightly so. There's no way on earth a cross word with her by someone would lead to her murder. Are you sure someone she knew did this disgusting thing?"

"No, but until we have formed a picture of her and her life, then this is all we have to begin our investigation."

"Okay, I think I comprehend that. It really hasn't sunk in yet. She was floating around the office this morning, so happy. It was her wedding anniversary, did you know?"

"Yes, we'd heard. So she had every reason to be happy if she loved her husband as much as we've been led to believe. What about the clients you deal with, anything there?"

He appeared momentarily puzzled by the question. "No, I wouldn't think so anyway. We're just a voice over the phone, how can anyone take umbrage with any of us?"

"It's something we need to investigate. You say she had a happy working and family life, but people don't get murdered just for the fun of it. Or maybe this is one such incident," Katy corrected herself, recollecting her own train of thought about this incident being a possible one-off.

"Shit! The thought of a madman walking the streets carrying a gun and taking pot shots at people just to get his kicks seems scary to me."

"Let's hope that isn't the case. However, so far, we haven't got any other clues to go on that would lead us to believe otherwise."

"I can't tell you anything else. She was a lovely person with no known enemies as far as I know."

"That's great. Okay, then we won't hold you up any longer. Would you like to send the next person in, please?"

"Sorry I couldn't be much help. I hope you find the person responsible and deal with the bastard appropriately."

"That's the plan. Nice to meet you, Steve."

He left the room.

Charlie stared down at her notes, or lack of them. "We're getting nowhere fast. Everyone seems to think she was a nice woman; she must have been to have paid Ben's rent for him when he was in dire straits. Not sure I know many people who would have volunteered to have done the same."

"Nope, me neither. Hopefully, the others will be able to throw a different light on things. If not, then we've got a fucking mammoth task ahead of us."

"Don't lose hope. We've got the forensic results to come back yet."

Katy smiled. "Thanks for the nudge, Charlie. You're right, we shouldn't give up hope just yet."

As it happened, Ben Thompson was the next work colleague to enter the room. "I'm Ben Thompson."

Katy nodded and introduced herself and Charlie. "You're only too aware of why we're here today, I presume?"

"Yes, to ask questions about what sort of person Grace was, am I right?" His green eyes sparkled with unshed tears.

"What can you tell us about Grace?"

"She was one of the kindest people I know. She bailed me out big time lately. Got me out of a financial hole and ended up keeping the roof over my head."

"Can you tell us about that?" Katy asked, already aware of what he was referring to, but she needed to ensure both his and Steve's stories matched up.

"My car broke down and needed a new engine. I didn't have the funds to cope with that and to meet my usual expenses. Grace saw I was down one day and called me into her office. I explained the situation and she…right there and then…offered to bail me out with enough money to keep my landlord off my back."

"That was kind of her."

"She was that type of lady. I was gobsmacked to be honest, she had a family of her own after all, and yet she didn't hesitate about coming to my aid."

"There aren't many people around like that, are there?"

"No, I guess there aren't. I paid her back, though. As soon as my bonus hit my bank account mid-month, it was the first thing I did. I couldn't stand the thought of having that debt over my head."

"Glad to hear it. I think I would be inclined to think along the same lines as you if it came down to it. Okay, we've already established she was a nice lady; did she get along with everyone here?"

"Oh yes, I believe so. If she didn't then she hid it well. Don't get me wrong, she wasn't a pushover to work for. She had very high standards and expected us to adhere to them or there would be trouble."

"Trouble? In what form would that present itself?"

"She wasn't afraid to issue a warning here and there if necessary. We took it from her, she used to be one of us and recently got promoted. Had an outsider come in and ordered us around like she had...well, they wouldn't have had the same impact, let's say that."

"I see. So no one took umbrage to her dishing out disciplinaries and the like then?"

"No. It was down to them to do their jobs properly in the first place, wasn't it?"

"Indeed. Did Grace ever have any problems with the punters—sorry, clients—she dealt with?"

"Not really. It was all phone-based, so it's easy to hang up on people if they start mouthing off, right?" He chuckled and straightened his face almost immediately.

"What about at home time? Did most of the staff leave together?"

"Yes, she rarely stayed behind because of getting home for the kids. If she had a long day ahead of her it usually began early as opposed to finishing late."

"And where do you tend to park?"

"There's an underground car park we use. I can't believe she's gone. She rarely goes out at lunchtime."

"We weren't aware of that. Such a shame she met her family today."

"A travesty, that's what it is. An absolute travesty for her to lose her life in such an evil way. My heart goes out to Toby and the kids. And just before Christmas, too. How sickening is that?"

"I agree. All right, if there's nothing else you can help us with, you're free to go."

"Can I take a card? If I think of anything later, maybe I could call you?"

Katy slid a card across the table. "I was about to suggest the same. Thanks for speaking with us."

"No problem. I hope Grace and her family get the justice they deserve and you find the evil shit who did this to her."

"So do we. We have to keep the faith and believe we will."

"Good luck. I wouldn't want your job if it was the last career going."

Katy smiled. "There are times we all feel the same about our chosen careers."

He left the room.

Charlie turned to Katy. "Really? Or were you saying that for his benefit?"

"You're new to the job, hon, there are bound to be days when you feel the same way. It's natural."

"Maybe. At the moment, my enthusiasm for the job is super high. I suppose there's a chance that will dwindle over time."

"It will, take my word for it."

Their conversation ended when a young tearful woman entered the room.

Katy welcomed her with a warm smile and gestured for her to take a seat. "Hello there, and you are?"

"Andrea Gregory. I was Grace's second-in-command if you like. You know, girls sticking together in a perceived man's world."

"Is it? Still? A tad old-fashioned scenario, isn't it?"

"Some men refuse to accept change. Not around here, I hasten to add. But out there, there are some clients who refuse to deal with a woman where their money is concerned. Maybe they think a woman is more likely to drop them in it with their wives, who knows? Sorry to be all doom and gloom, that comes from having too much time on my hands. I've been trying to think if anyone Grace has dealt with lately would have it in them to make an attempt on her life…you know…kill her. You're sure to ask me that, right?"

"You're correct. Did you manage to come up with anything?"

"No, not really. Not in the last three months or so. Back in June, there was a shitty incident with an investor who lost thousands. He rang Grace shouting the odds at her. She took it all on board like we're supposed to, the customer being right and all that, until she'd had enough and refused to take any more from him. He went on and on at her until she produced an email in which she advised him not to be too foolhardy with his money. That shut him up for a few minutes, then he demanded to be transferred to Colin and put in a complaint about her. Colin ignored the man to an extent, sort of. He listened to him, took down his details, revisited the account and correspondence Grace had with him over the previous months and saw nothing wrong. The man was smarting, livid because he'd lost so much money and was reaching out for someone to blame other than his own stupidity." Her head dipped after she'd finished. "Why? I'm not saying it was him, but some madman did this to her. Who and why?"

"That's what we're doing our best to comprehend. Do you have a name for this person and his address?"

"I can get it for you."

"If you would."

Andrea tore out of the room and returned a few moments later with a name and address written on a piece of paper which she placed in Charlie's outstretched hand.

Charlie wrote the details in her notebook and handed back the sheet of paper. "Thanks, I've got that now."

"You're welcome. I'm in no way apportioning blame here. All I was doing was trying to figure out if there was someone who had any cause for complaint and he was the only one who came to mind."

Katy leaned over to read what Charlie had entered into the book. "Gordon Brightman. Hmm…he lives in a posh area. Can I ask how much he lost?"

"I'm not sure if I can divulge that information. Maybe I should check with Colin first, sorry."

"Don't be. I can get a warrant if necessary, this is a murder inquiry after all."

Andrea peered over her shoulder and back to Katy. "It was over a million."

Katy whistled. "But you told us it was a few thousand."

"I know. I was stretching the truth a little."

"Wow, no wonder he was livid."

Andrea shrugged. "Toying with the stock market can be a risky business, take my word for it. What I didn't tell you was he'd made a killing on the market the year before. That's why he came back for more and used a larger sum. It doesn't always work out that way, the markets can be volatile at the best of times."

"Surely people know that. I steer clear of it for that very reason, not that I have much spare cash to splurge. Everyone knows their money is at risk, don't they?"

"They should do. I suppose with some people if they have success their greed gene starts crying out for more. I didn't like the man. He sounded a bolshy bugger over the phone, if you get my drift. I was in the office when he began yelling at Grace; it was awful. No one should be allowed to get away with speaking to someone like that in business, or everyday life come to that, either. Disgusting little man."

"Can I ask what Colin did about the complaint?"

"He went back to the man and told him to take it higher, to the ombudsman, if necessary, because as far as he could see Grace had done nothing wrong."

"And did Mr Brightman do that?"

"I don't know, you'll have to ask Colin. Although these types of complaints can take months to come through, so I'm led to believe, not that we've had to deal with that many, not during my time here. Some people need to get a life. If you had the money, would you take a punt with a million quid? I know I wouldn't."

Katy sighed. "If I had that sort of money, I would be using it wisely, like buying a boat and taking my family around the Med and farther afield. I'd leave all the criminals in the UK far behind me. Ah, a girl can dream."

The three of them chuckled.

"Exactly, you wouldn't gamble it trying to make more money for you, would you?" Andrea stated.

"No, I don't think I would, but people have different needs and desires in this life. Has he been in touch since, to invest more money?"

"No. He told Grace, in an unkind manner, where she could stick her advice and that he would be taking his portfolio of investments elsewhere. We haven't heard from him since that call."

"We'll chase it up once we leave here. So are you telling us that you were close to Grace?"

"Very. We confided in each other a lot, being the only women on the team."

"Perhaps she confided about her personal life, did she?"

"Yes and no. All I know is that she adored her husband and her kids." Her words came out strained, and a few tears flowed.

"I'm sorry. I didn't mean to upset you."

"You haven't. The killer did that when he took her life. Are none of us safe these days? She was so looking forward to spending time with her family Christmas shopping, it was a rarity for her to have a full lunch hour. She could usually be found at her desk, munching on a sandwich while she continued to work. I was so pleased to see her away from her desk and happy at the thought of her going out for lunch...and then this happened."

"It's very sad. So this was a novelty, you say, her going out for lunch?"

"Yes, definitely."

Katy nodded as the cogs started churning. *Therefore, the crime couldn't have been premeditated unless the killer targeting Grace was unaware of what her routine was.* "Okay, that's given us another line of enquiry to rattle down. Can you think of anything else untoward that has happened over the past few months?"

"No, not really. Grace and I were truly excited about her obtaining her promotion. She was about to set a few things in motion to change certain criteria that would be less restrictive to a woman's ability in the workplace."

41

Katy inclined her head. "Things that might have stirred up a hornet's nest, perhaps?"

"Undoubtedly. It's a shame she hadn't instigated anything before her death." Her head dipped again.

"Were any of the other team members privy to the plans she wanted to introduce?"

"No. It was privileged information between the two of us. I would never have let on to anyone, not before she'd implemented them."

"So people weren't likely to take umbrage at something they didn't know about?"

"No. Truly, they weren't anything major, just slight tweaks which might have stepped on a few toes, nothing more than that. Even if they felt they had been put in place, I couldn't see anyone going out of their way..."

Shouts and cries for help broke out in the hallway.

Katy raced out there to find the other team members darting around like headless chickens. "What is it? What's going on?"

Ben and Steve were standing outside Colin's office, just pointing, their mouths hung open in stunned silence.

3

*K*aty pushed past them and into the room. "Shit!" she murmured. "Charlie, get in here," she bellowed.

She made her way over to the man stretched out on the floor beside his desk. Blood pooling into the grey carpet surrounding him from two wounds; one to his head and the other to his chest. Katy felt for a pulse even though she could tell he was dead by the way his glazed eyes stared at her.

"Fuck!" Charlie cried from the doorway.

"Get them back, put them in another office and call for backup. No, forget that, I'll do it. Just get them out of here."

"Come on, guys, you don't want to see this." Charlie ushered the two men away from the door.

"What's going on?" Andrea asked.

"It's Colin. He's been shot," Ben advised her, his voice trembling.

"Come on, stay back. Is there a room we can use that has no windows?" Charlie asked.

"Yes, at the end of the hall," Andrea replied.

Charlie motioned for one of the men to lead the way.

Once they had all moved from the doorway, Katy fished out her mobile and called the station. "Hi, Mick, it's DI Foster. I need another set of officers at Zedex, there's been a shooting."

"Shit! Want me to call an ambulance?"

"Nope, it would be a waste of time. I'll ring them in a moment after I've called the pathologist. Just get a team over here pronto. Are your guys still at the scene down below?"

"Yes, they were just packing up. I can reappoint them to you now."

"No, leave them in situ. What the fuck is going on? How does someone take a pot shot at someone when there's a police presence at the scene already?"

"They're either brave or stupid. I'll get this actioned immediately, ma'am."

"Thanks." She ended the call and moved over to the window, back against the wall, edging alongside it to peer out, cautious that the killer might still be out there, ready to take another shot at any time. A few rooftops on the opposite side of the street were visible as well as possibly a couple of hundred windows to choose from where the shooter could have taken a shot from.

"Don't get too close," Charlie warned from the doorway.

"Jesus, you scared the crap out of me. Are the staff all right?"

Charlie walked into the office and kept to the edge of the room to join her. "They're shaken up. How could this happen with us here?"

"You tell me. Uniformed police down below as well. I need to ring Patti, get her and Forensics back here."

Katy stepped away from the window, and Charlie swapped places with her.

Katy tugged on her arm. "Not too close. The last thing I need right now is to train up yet another partner."

"You can't get rid of me that easily. I'll be careful." Charlie turned back to survey the area.

"Hi, Patti, it's me, and no, I'm not going to start pestering you. You need to get back here."

"What? We've only just got back to base. Why? Did we miss something?"

"There's been another murder. Grace's boss has been shot."

"What the fuck? Okay, I'll gather the team and be there within twenty to thirty minutes." Patti hung up before Katy could say anything else.

"She's on her way."

"All I can see is a lot of windows as possible vantage points from which to take the shot," Charlie said as Katy joined her.

"Don't forget the roofs as well. Any one of those could have been used. I get the feeling the killer has been within spitting distance of us all along, waiting to pounce again, to seize another opportunity, but why?"

"Two executives from the same firm, there has to be more to it." Charlie shook her head.

"Yeah, we need to get the team out here. Start asking probing questions, shake a few trees if we have to."

"I'll get on it, if you like?"

"Take it in the hallway, Charlie."

"Will do."

Charlie left her position, which allowed Katy to get closer to the window. Her gaze was drawn to one roof in particular opposite. She saw something or someone move. Yes, it was a person. She sprinted out of the office and called the lift. The security guy was beside himself, pacing the hallway, as much use as a chocolate teapot left out in the midday sun.

He was mumbling the same words over and over, "I should've kept them both safe…it was my responsibility and I screwed up."

"Don't be daft. You haven't screwed up. Just guard the lift, make sure anyone who comes up here shows you the relevant ID. I've summoned the pathologist and the Forensics team—do not let anyone else off the lift, except me, of course. Are you armed?"

He took out a truncheon and a pepper spray. "With this."

"It'll have to do. Just aim it in the person's eyes."

"Don't worry, I'm aware of where to use it."

Katy smiled and pressed the ground-floor button. She dashed out of the lift once it had reached its destination and tore through the reception area and past the uniformed officers outside. "Has the desk sergeant been in touch yet?"

The young officer closest to her nodded. "Yes, he told us there'd been another shooting. What do you need us to do, ma'am?"

"Man the doors. Don't let anyone into the building unless they're one of our associates, got that?"

"Yes, ma'am. Where are you going?"

"Never you mind. Just do your job and keep people away from the area," she called over her shoulder.

By now, the traffic was flowing once more. Katy picked a path through the moving vehicles and then darted along the pavement, searching for an entry point into the building she'd highlighted. There it was. She entered the main door and jumped on board the lift which took her to the tenth floor. The bell pinged, and the doors whooshed open. She exited and hunted the corridor for a possible entrance that would lead her up to the roof. Finally, she spotted a door and eased it open. She knew she was taking a risk going it alone. Maybe she'd regret her actions in the future. For now, she would press on. The corridor lit up as soon as she entered. Withdrawing her Taser from her pocket, she ascended the stairs. She pushed against the fire door, and it sprang open. She ran onto the roof and hunkered down. Shielded by a low wall, Katy surged forward. Footsteps sounded on the other side of the wall. She squeezed her eyes shut for a split second. After realising that was a foolish action, she opened them again to find a masked man standing in front of her. She aimed her Taser. He kicked it out of her hand and rammed the butt of his rifle into her chest and then her head.

Everything went black…

*K*aty woke up and groggily got to her feet. She picked up her Taser and scoured the area. The masked man was long gone. Her legs gave way beneath her. She eased herself onto the wall and dialled Charlie's number. "I need help."

"What? Where are you?"

"Are you still in Colin's office?"

"Yes. Why?"

"Look out the window. The building opposite with ten storeys. I'm on the roof." Katy waved her arms, hoping that Charlie would be able to see her from where she was standing.

"I've got you. Stay there, I'm on my way."

"No. Send one of the men. You stay there. The killer attacked me, he could still be around here."

"Shit! Okay, I'll send someone now. Shall I call an ART to attend?"

"Maybe that would be the wisest option, I should have made the call before. Damn, I was out cold. I'm disorientated, Charlie. I can't think straight."

"On it now. Can you stay there? Don't move, I have you in sight, I'll keep an eye on you from here."

"I'll stay here. Hurry. I feel sick. I'd hate to pass out and choke on my vomit."

"Ewww...did you have to say that? Let me get back to you. Stay put."

Katy jabbed at the End Call button and sucked in a couple of deep breaths to settle her queasy stomach. It temporarily helped until the bile rose in her throat again a few seconds later. She scanned the area for a possible outside tap—there wasn't one. She inhaled a few more breaths, and the sensation dipped again, only to surge once more a few seconds later.

A little while passed then her phone rang. "Charlie, is that you?"

"It is. Help is on its way. Stay put for five minutes. I had to go by the book on this one, boss. I rang DCI Roberts to check what to do."

"Great. Okay, the damage has been done now. I ain't moving anytime soon."

"Sorry if I made the wrong call. I was out of my depth."

"Don't apologise, you did what you had to do. I'd rather you do that than screw things up...oh God..." Katy emptied her stomach and kept retching for the next few seconds until she was able to speak again. "I'm okay, it'll pass. Don't worry about me."

"Of course I'm worried. I wish I was there with you."

"I don't. This fucker could still be around..."

"No, don't say that. I can't see anyone from here. Just stay safe and alert."

"I'm trying my best."

"Don't hang up, keep the line open. Patti is here now. I've seen her arrive down below. Wait, yes, the ART are here now as well. They'll be with you soon."

"Thanks, Charlie. You've done good. I'll buy you a cream cake... oh God, did I have to mention food?"

"Hang in there. Rid your mind of cream et cetera."

Katy vomited again. She'd never felt so ill in all her life. Well, maybe throughout her pregnancy, but the morning sickness soon passed after a few months of discomfort. It was the dizziness overpowering her that she found hard to bear.

"Are you okay?" Charlie shouted, concerned.

"I will be soon. Are they on their way in?"

"They're on the roof. I can see them approaching you now. Shout out to them, Katy."

"Here, I'm over here," Katy called out.

Four armed policemen dashed towards her.

One dropped to his knee, avoiding the vomit. "Are you all right?"

She pointed at the pile of sick beside him. "Sorry about that, I couldn't keep it down. I think I'm all right. My legs are wobbly, so standing is out of the question."

"We'll help you. What about the assailant?"

"I don't know. He knocked me out. When I regained consciousness he was gone—at least I think he's gone."

"Stay there. We'll do a quick recce of the area and then get you to safety."

"I appreciate it."

One officer remained by her side while the three others set off in different directions. They returned moments later.

"There's no one here," one of the men said, and the other two agreed.

The officer who had narrowly avoided what she'd had for lunch placed a hand on her elbow and helped her to her feet. She wavered slightly, and her vision blurred.

"I feel bloody drunk—no, it's far worse than that."

"We'll get you some medical attention soon, I believe an ambulance has been called."

"No, I don't want to waste anyone's time. I'll be fine after a sit-down."

"I doubt it. You seem concussed. You're going to need to go to the hospital."

"Damn, not what I want to hear."

"Tough, it's a necessity. We can't have an inspector on duty, vomiting while she questions possible witnesses, now can we?"

"I'd laugh at that if I had it in me. Don't make me chuckle, please."

He snorted. "I'll try not to. Jed, take the other side, let's get this young lady back downstairs."

"Young lady? You old charmer. Hey, I'm a married woman, you know?"

"He's a lucky man. What am I saying? I'm a married man, so we're quits, right?"

Katy attempted a smile, and it came out more of a grimace.

The four men, two in front and one on either side of her, accompanied her down the flight of stairs and into the lift.

"Shit! Not an ideal travelling mode when your guts are doing dozens of somersaults."

"I know. Try not to think about it and breathe," the officer in charge said.

The lift hit the bottom, and the men swiftly left the cavity and transported her outside.

"Thank you, I'll be fine now. My partner is here, she'll take care of me."

The four men nodded and hopped into their vehicle.

"My knights in shining armour are now departing," Katy mumbled.

"You look rough. Hospital with you, and no arguments."

"What a waste, calling for an ambulance. I'm all right, honestly!" Katy turned to look over her shoulder and swiftly lost her balance.

Charlie rushed to hold her upright and prevent her from bashing into a nearby wall. "Never kid a kidder, as Mum has been known to say. Don't fight me on this one, boss."

A young female paramedic came to their assistance. "How are you doing?"

"I'm fine." Katy beamed, eager to brush off her dizzy spells.

"Hmm…you don't look fine. Let's get you in the back of the ambulance and run a few tests."

Katy sighed and puffed out her cheeks. "If you insist. I'm not one to argue with authority."

"Bullshit," Charlie said on a cough, earning her a dig in the ribs.

The paramedic helped Katy into the back of the ambulance.

"Should I call AJ?" Charlie asked.

"No. Definitely *not*. I swear I'll be fine in a little while. Jesus, you need to leave me and get on with the case, Charlie. Someone needs to tell Colin's next of kin before they hear about it through the media. Send Stephen and Patrick, tell them to be compassionate."

"Should I need to tell them that?"

"Whatever. Just do it."

Charlie raced off, and Katy let out a long breath.

"You can stop the pretence now," the paramedic whispered in her ear. "How do you really feel?"

"Like my head, and my legs come to that, belong to someone else. I'm disorientated and don't know what to do for the best. Sit down, stand up, lean against something to support me."

"That's all natural. You definitely have concussion. We're going to take you in. Who's AJ?"

"My husband," she replied quietly. "Please, I don't want to worry him, it's an important day for him and his business. What's your name?"

"Angie. I understand, but surely he'd want to know if you've been injured."

"He would, but he's a worrywart. Leave things as they are for now. I promise to ring him after a doctor has given me the once-over."

Charlie reappeared at the back of the ambulance. "That's sorted. I've told the guys I'll be coming with you."

"No, Charlie, I don't want a fuss. You stay here."

Charlie shook her head. "Sorry, boss, this is one order that I refuse to comply with."

Angie laughed. "I love a bit of insubordination. She's right, someone should be with you. Do you want to follow us in your car?"

Charlie held out her hand for Katy's keys. "Good idea. Are you setting off now?"

"We are. The sooner the doctor assesses her the better."

"I now know what someone being bullied feels like," Katy grumbled.

Charlie and Angie laughed.

"As if," Charlie replied.

Within ten minutes, the ambulance pulled up outside the Accident and Emergency department, and Charlie joined Katy again once she'd parked the car. Katy was wheeled through to triage on a stretcher. Luckily, there were only a few minor injuries to contend with before it was her turn to be seen by the doctor.

A good-looking male doctor in his early thirties examined her under Charlie's watchful gaze at Katy's request.

He carried out a series of tests on her which covered her speech, memory, balance, hearing and vision. Thankfully, Katy passed all the tests with ease.

"Don't get too carried away," the doctor warned. "I need you to have a CT scan, we're organising that now."

"But everything else is fine. I'm feeling better with every passing minute," Katy complained, feeling like a fraud as her results had proved there was no significant impact.

The doctor raised an eyebrow. "Are you? No BS, Inspector."

"I'm not, I swear. The urge to vomit has dissipated, and I'm thinking far more clearly than I was after I regained consciousness. I don't want to put you to too much trouble."

"You're not. It's a necessity to see what's going on in that head of yours. If the whack was hard enough to knock you out then you're going to have to accept how important it is to find out what's happening in there."

"Come on, boss, what harm can it do? I'd want to know," Charlie said, quick to jump in.

"Okay, stop badgering me, the pair of you. I'm telling you I'm fine, though. You're the ones intent on wasting funds, not me."

"It's not a waste of funds. There's a limit to what we can do without science getting involved. I'll get it organised and be back in a moment. Stay there, don't move, and yes, that's an order."

He left her bedside, and Katy crossed her arms in defiance.

"Have I told you how much I detest hospitals?"

"Yeah, Mum was the same. She's had her fair share of scares over the years."

"I remember most of them well. How's her stomach now after the crazed mare stabbed her?"

"It's healed up nicely. She gets a niggle from the wound now and again but basically she's made of strong stuff, but you know that, right?"

Katy grinned. "We're from the same mould, love. I can't help feeling frustrated. That bastard has got away again. Two murders in one day, and he came and went like a bloody ghost or something. Was he there all along? Lying in wait?"

"Don't start blaming yourself, Katy. We couldn't have known where the shots that took Grace out came from. Had we known they'd come from the roof of the building opposite we would have checked it out, wouldn't we?"

"I know. That sort of thing doesn't filter down the line for a few days, not until the Forensic team have run their tests and analysed things thoroughly. You wait, when I get my hands on the bastard who did this to me, you're going to have to restrain me."

Charlie sniggered. "I figured that might be the case. I'll take that on board, because we will find him. Okay, don't have a go at me here, but the question has to be asked: why didn't he kill you? Why did he choose to knock you out cold and leave you on that roof, when he could have either killed you or even abducted you? That part doesn't make sense to me."

Katy frowned as she contemplated Charlie's observations. "I don't have the answers to that. The thought hadn't even crossed my mind. I suppose I should be grateful to him or her, we haven't established the killer's gender yet."

"True enough."

The doctor rejoined them. "The porter will take you down for your scan now."

"Can Charlie come with me?"

He nodded and smiled warmly. "Of course. Partners in all you do, right?" He winked.

Charlie's mouth dropped open.

Katy burst out laughing. "Professionally speaking, yes."

"Ah, sorry. My mistake," the doctor replied, his cheeks turning crimson.

Luckily, the porter arrived to spare him any further embarrassment. He pushed Katy through the narrow corridors and deposited her at the X-ray department where she went straight through to have the scan. Charlie remained outside in the waiting room. The whole thing was over in a matter of minutes, and the porter returned to take her back to A&E.

It was another half an hour or so before she received the results.

The doctor entered the cubicle and smiled. "Maybe a mild concussion. No lasting damage done, and yes, you're free to go."

"That's wonderful news. I feel so much better than I did an hour ago. See, I told you I didn't want to make a fuss. Would you guys listen to me? No."

Charlie shook her head, leaned towards the doctor and said, "See what I have to put up with? She's always right, or thinks she is."

The three of them laughed.

"It was nice meeting you, ladies. Hopefully we won't have the pleasure of meeting again anytime soon."

"We'll take care of each other from now on, I promise," Katy replied. She placed her legs on the floor and prepared to wobble.

Instead, she remained steady on her feet. Another blessing in disguise. "Come on, partner, we have a killer to catch."

"Whoa! Who said anything about you being fit to return to work?" The doctor tutted and shook his head. "My advice would be to take the rest of the day off and see how you feel in the morning."

Katy began to object, but his raised hand cut her off. "Okay, you win. I'll go home and put my feet up."

"Very wise." He smiled and left the cubicle.

"Like I'm going to listen to him."

"Do I have to report back to DCI Roberts?" Charlie warned.

Katy scowled. "You wouldn't dare."

"I might if you push me into a corner."

"Ha, so much for loyalty. I sense a call to your mother in the near future."

"Okay, joking aside. You should take the rest of the day off, it's only a couple of hours before the end of our shift."

"Not when we have the likes of this fucker on the loose, Charlie. I'll be fine. End of. You drive, just in case."

"I can see it would be pointless arguing the toss with you. Where are we going?"

"Back to Zedex. I need to have a chat with Patti, make sure we're both on the same page with this one. She needs to get us the results ASAP before he strikes again."

"You think he will?"

"Yep. Don't you?"

Charlie inserted the key into the ignition and shrugged. "I'm not so sure. It's looking more and more like someone who had a grudge with the firm."

"My thoughts exactly. We need to find out who that person could be and question the staff again."

"If they're up to it."

Charlie drove them back to what had become another crowd-pulling scene. *What the fuck? They must have heard the shots. Why the heck would they remain in the area if there's a gunman on the loose?*

"Can we get these people back and away from here?" she instructed the uniformed copper on site.

"Yes, come on, guys. This is still a crime scene, and we haven't caught the perp yet, so they could still be around, ready to take another shot at someone. Let's bear that in mind and get these people shifted, like now," Katy added.

"I'll see what I can do, ma'am," the young male constable replied. He whistled for a couple of his colleagues to join him.

Katy and Charlie left them to it and jumped into the lift to take them to the top floor. Patti made a beeline for them as soon as they entered the room.

Katy pre-empted the pathologist's lecture. "Please, don't make a fuss. I'm all right. I've been checked over, and the doctor gave me the go-ahead to carry on working."

Patti's eyes narrowed, and she reached out to touch the large lump that had emerged on Katy's forehead. "Why don't I believe you? Charlie, tell me the truth or I'll get on the phone to your mother…"

Katy tutted. "Don't use emotional blackmail on her. Don't you have any respect, woman? I'm fine. I've got a slight bump, so what? I've also got a fucker of a villain to capture. You'd do exactly the same if you were in my position, and don't try to ruddy well deny it, either."

Patti inclined her head. "Wow, feisty bitch when you want to be, aren't you?"

"I am. I'm no longer living in Lorne Simpkins' shadow, so if you wouldn't mind showing me the same respect you've shown her over the years, I'd appreciate it. Shall we get back to the dastardly crime now? Wait, before you give me a mouthful of abuse, have SOCO been dispatched to the roof over the road?"

"Yes, they're there now. All right, I won't bother laying into you, it's your life after all. Just remember it's not just your life at stake if something bad happens to you, you have AJ and Georgie to consider as well."

"I'm aware of that, which is the main reason I wanted to get back to work. AJ has a big day ahead of him and…"

"You're wrong, so wrong. But that's my two pennies' worth. It's your life we're discussing here, not mine."

Katy circled her head, and her neck clicked several times. "Are you done now?"

"I am. Right, with the second victim being shot from the roof, we're now presuming that Grace Hunt was targeted from the same area. The question is, why? Why kill two people working for the same firm?"

"Two important members of the firm at that," Katy added.

Patti crossed her arms and placed a pointed finger against her cheek. "Are we thinking along the lines of revenge or possibly talking about someone with a grudge?"

"That's at the top of my list, yes," Katy admitted.

"Did the staff have anything to say after the first murder?"

"We were in the process of interviewing the last person when we were alerted to Colin's death. None of the staff could think of anything other than a possible investor who had lost a million in the market crash. I suppose we should call on him, find out what he has to say about things. His name was Gordon something, wasn't it?"

Charlie flipped through her notebook and nodded. "Gordon Bright-man. I'll see if Andrea can tell me anything else about him."

Patti watched Charlie leave the room. "She's good, I can tell. Not that there were any doubts, knowing who her mother is. I miss not having Lorne around but I think her daughter is a suitable stand-in, don't you?"

"Sort of. She's already read me the riot act today. If I'd shut my eyes, I swear it could have been Lorne giving me a tongue-lashing."

"Ouch! That bad? And then you come here and I start on you. Not what you want when recovering from concussion, I take it?"

"Nope, you've got that right. No, in all seriousness, we need to pull out all the stops to track this shithead down, Patti, and not just because he walloped me one and left me with a sore head either. Two murders within hours of each other. Why? Who does a shitty thing like that?"

"And where did the weapon come from?"

"That's the least of my worries. He would've had to have got it from underground resources. All we have to find out is where and how?"

"Good luck with that one. Maybe a member of your team can put the word out on the street to obtain a lead."

"Yeah, a couple of them have good contacts on the streets, it's worth seeing if they know anything. Other than that, we have nothing. The guy was wearing a mask when I confronted him, so even if we manage to pick him up on CCTV cameras, I reckon he'll have worn the mask to have entered the area and not taken it off until he was well clear of here."

"Nothing wrong with the way your brain is functioning then."

"I told you, I'm fine."

Charlie came bounding into the room again, as eager as a child on a promise. "Nope, nothing else. Should we go over there and check the guy out?"

"We should. If Patti hasn't got anything else for us?"

"I haven't, now get out of my hair. Both of you."

"Keep me informed on this one, Patti, especially the forensics side of things because I feel that's going to be imperative in breaking the case wide open."

"I will. Trust me. Just take care of yourself. Charlie, on your head be it if she suffers a relapse."

Charlie's eyes widened. "Wow, really? Why should I be to blame? I tried talking her out of coming back to work, but she was having none of it. But thanks for blaming me if she cocks up."

Patti nudged Katy. "Yep, just like her mother, bites before she engages her brain."

Katy and Patti laughed while Charlie harumphed and left the room.

4

*A*s it happened, they had two addresses for Gordon Brightman. His home and his work addresses. Katy took a punt and instructed Charlie to drive to the warehouse from where he ran his export business.

The noise of the forklift trucks shifting pallets around the large warehouse gave Katy a thumping headache. She winced and closed her eyes.

"Shit, are you all right?" Charlie asked.

"I will be if we can get away from the blasted machinery."

A woman appeared at the doorway to an office over to the left. "Hey, you shouldn't be in here, not without the proper safety get-up on."

Katy and Charlie crossed the warehouse to join her.

Katy flashed her ID. "Sorry, we need to have a chat with Gordon Brightman, if he's here."

"He's out back, watching over the goods being loaded. Can I ask why you need to speak with him?"

"It's personal. Is there somewhere we can wait? Could someone take over from him?"

"No. He oversees all the loading. He'd go with the driver and watch the goods being unloaded at the other end if he could. Come through to the office. I'll go and have a word, see if he can spare you five minutes or so. The delay shouldn't matter too much. He won't be happy, though. Just warning you."

"Do your best. Before you go, has he been here all morning?"

The secretary chewed on her lip and thought it over. "Yes, although he did pop out earlier for an hour or two."

"Did he say where?"

"On a personal mission, he told me. I won't be long. Take a seat." She scooted past them, rushed through the warehouse and disappeared through a door at the back.

Katy and Charlie sat on the two spare chairs in the room.

They didn't have to wait long until a rotund man in his fifties came into the office, his secretary not far behind him. "I'm Gordon Brightman, you wanted a word with me?"

Katy presented her warrant card again. "DI Katy Foster and DC Charlie Simpkins. If you don't mind. Is there somewhere private we can have a chat?"

"Yep, come this way. I can only spare you five minutes, though. I have a hectic schedule today."

"That's fine."

He opened the door behind where Katy was sitting, and she and Charlie followed him into another tight office, boxes piled high in one corner and a desk with a computer in the other.

He removed two chairs from a stack and placed them in front of his desk. "Now, what's all this about?"

"Between the hours of one and three today, where were you?"

"Here. Loading wagons, it's our busiest day. Why?"

"Your secretary said you went out this morning for a while. May I ask where you went?"

"Out on personal business. That is allowed, isn't it? Or is that a criminal offence nowadays?"

"It's allowed. Can I ask what sort of business, sir?"

"I went to book a holiday as a surprise for my wife's fiftieth birthday which is coming up next month." He bent down and opened the briefcase lying on the floor by his desk. He threw the tickets at her. "There, see. Two tickets to Mexico. First-class accommodation and flights."

"Thank you. Your wife is lucky to have such a thoughtful husband."

"She is. I appreciate her as much as she appreciates me. We both work hard. She's a barrister."

"I see. And she agrees with your dealings with Zedex?"

His brow pinched into tight lines. "What do they have to do with anything?"

"Answer the question, if you would," Katy prompted.

"She knows briefly that I invest."

"Is she aware you recently lost a large sum of money on the stock exchange?"

His cheeks reddened under Katy's intense gaze. "No, she's not aware of that. She has no need to hear about it either. It was my personal money I invested and lost on that deal."

Katy probed further. "I see. You were angry about losing the vast sum, weren't you?"

He inhaled and exhaled several large breaths and glared at Katy. "Too right I was. Wouldn't you be?"

"Not really, because I wouldn't have gambled that much money in the first place."

"I'm a businessman, my whole business is about taking risks in one form or another. Every firm either lives or dies by the owner's ability to take a gamble now and again, I can assure you."

"Sir, there's no need to be so defensive."

"Sorry. It's still very raw."

"Am I to understand that you blamed Zedex for losing that money for you?"

"One person in particular more like. The bitch who took over my account and screwed up."

Katy tilted her head. "Harsh words for someone you should have trusted."

"It's the truth. She didn't know what the hell she was doing. I used to deal with someone else there, but he upped and left. I have no idea why. I was told that Hunt woman was the best the firm had, therefore I had to go with her. I've regretted my decision ever since. She was hopeless. Before I realised what was going on, my bank balance was a million quid lighter, go figure."

"Sorry to hear that. Can you tell me why the other member of staff left?"

"I don't know. You'll have to ask them the ins and outs of that. James was a good lad, we got on great. I wish I'd stayed in touch with him, but one minute he was there, and the next he'd gone. I tried to get it out of that Hunt woman, you know, tried to get his address so I could stay in contact with him, but she refused to hand it over. Spouted about data protection which is a load of twaddle. Anyway, I don't understand what this has to do with you being here today, so please do enlighten me."

"Earlier today, two people at Zedex were killed."

"What? You're kidding me? How?" His eyes widened as it appeared to dawn on him why they were there. "No way! You're not going to try and pin this on me, are you?"

"If you have an alibi, then no, we won't. But there is still a grievance we need to look into."

"Why? I lost a lot of wedge, dosh, mazuma, whatever you want to call it. That's the end of the line for me. If you think I would take some form of revenge then you're gravely mistaken. I'll just knuckle down and make another million to replace the one I unwisely lost. That's my revenge, so to speak. Fancy them being killed. Who was it, do I know them?"

"The first was Grace Hunt, and the second was her boss, Colin Markham."

He let out a low whistle. "Wow, do you think someone in a similar position to mine did this to them, is that why you're here?"

"Possibly. It's an avenue we need to go down first and foremost. Did you have much to do with Colin?"

"No, not really. I mean, yes, he listened to my complaint and analysed it but he deemed the transaction was above board and that the crash of the companies I backed couldn't have been foreseen. The usual jargon, I felt at the time."

"It did nothing to quell the anger you felt, though?"

"Not really. I've since learned to live with it. Like I said, I'm the type to knuckle down and get on with making my next million. I'm a quarter of the way there already." He glanced at his watch. "So, if you'll excuse me, time is money and all that. Never a truer word spoken, I can tell you."

"Okay, we'll leave it there for now. We may have reason to revisit you in the future if we have any more queries for you."

"Feel free. And for the record, I'm sorry they're both dead. I wouldn't want to wish that on anyone, no matter what I personally felt about them."

"Good to hear. Thank you for sparing us the time. You can get back to making your fortune again now."

"Thanks. I'll do just that."

He showed them out, walking them across the warehouse safely to their car. He then waved them off and turned towards the wagons being loaded.

"What do you think?" Katy slipped back into the car.

Charlie faced her. "Is this another test?"

Katy smiled. "If you want to call it that, yes."

"I thought he was genuine enough. Did you notice the shock on his face when you revealed who the victims were?"

"I did. Therefore, I'm willing to cross him off our list of suspects after his alibi has been confirmed."

They drove back to the station, pulling into the car park as Patrick and Stephen arrived.

"Hey, how did it go?" Katy asked.

Patrick shook his head. "Terrible. I mean, we were really compassionate when we told Colin's wife that her husband wouldn't be coming home, but she bloody melted down all the same. I don't think either of us was prepared for her sorrowful reaction." His eyes watered.

Katy patted his arm. "Sorry you guys had to deal with that. You never know how the grieving families are going to react."

"Glad that task is usually down to you, that's all I can say," Patrick replied with a glimmer of a smile. "How's the head?"

"The doctor gave me the all-clear to return to work, so let's crack on."

Patrick shot Charlie a look. "She did?"

"No, she didn't. But Katy's the boss. I'm not about to start telling her what's right and wrong, I need this job."

They all laughed and entered the building.

For the next hour, Katy and the team brought the whiteboard up to date and bounced around a few ideas. They listed Gordon Brightman as a possible suspect, then Katy had second thoughts and struck his name off the list again.

"That's it. Not sure where we go from here until we get word back from the lab regarding any DNA or evidence likely found at the two locations, the murder scene of victim one, and the rooftop where I spotted the killer."

"Where he attacked you, you mean," Charlie corrected, shaking her head.

"All right, there's no need to rub it in. I say we call it a day and pick things up again in the morning. Carry out all the background checks and scour the CCTV footage, to try and find something that might help us. The thing is, even if we manage to locate something, the killer wore a mask, I know that first-hand."

"But he'll have needed to have used a vehicle to get to the location," Charlie piped up.

"True enough. One last thing, if any of you have contacts on the street, now would be a good time to get in touch with them. That weapon must have come from somewhere. All right, come on, pack up and get out of here."

The rest of the team drifted off, leaving Katy and Charlie to switch off the lights.

On the way down the concrete stairs, Charlie said, "Do you need me to take you home?"

"No. You worry too much. I promise to take a leisurely ride home so I don't put my brain under too much strain. I know that'll be a novelty for me."

Charlie snorted. "You're nuts. You took two fair old whacks today, and look at you, apart from the huge bump extending on your forehead, no one would know. You amaze me with your tenacity and willingness not to give in."

"Thanks, I've always prided myself on getting on with the job in hand, no matter what diversions stand in my way. Your mother was the same. Maybe that's where I acquired it from."

"Yeah, she's a stubborn lady most of the time. It was sure to rub off on you, eventually."

Katy smiled and slipped into her vehicle. "I'll see you in the morning."

Charlie held the door open. "Promise me if you feel rough, you'll take a sickie."

"I will. Enjoy what's left of your evening, hon."

"You, too. Send my love to Georgie and AJ. I hope he's not too heavy-handed with you."

Katy held up her crossed fingers and started the engine. Charlie slammed the door shut, and when Katy glanced back in her rear-view mirror, Charlie was still standing in the same spot staring after her. *Bless her, she's such a caring soul, just like Lorne.*

"What in God's name is that?" AJ shouted the moment he saw her. He was standing at the cooker, stirring a pot of bolognaise sauce, one of his specialities which Katy adored.

She left the kitchen and returned wearing a frown. "Where's madam?"

"I asked a question first, Katy, stop avoiding the bloody huge elephant in the room."

"Don't have a go at me, AJ. Do that, and you won't get anything out of me."

He marched towards her and gripped the tops of her arms. His voice softened. "It's only because I care."

"I know you do, but there are ways of talking to your wife if you want an honest response."

He kissed her on the lips and then gently touched the bruised skin around the large swelling. "Who hurt my baby?"

"A madman. You're lucky I'm still alive." As soon as the words left her mouth, she regretted saying them. Her eyes closed, and she braced herself for the barrage she feared was on the way.

Instead, AJ reached for her hand and led her to the kitchen table. He pulled out two chairs, and they both sank into them.

"I'm angry because I care. I'm not apportioning blame, love, you should know that by now."

"I do and I love you even more for being the kind and supportive husband you are. Honestly, I'm fine. A little concussion, that's all."

"What? Don't tell me you drove yourself home?"

"Okay, I won't." She smiled and touched his cheek. "Don't have a go, please. It's been an exceptionally hard day. Two murders, and me being within an inch of the killer..." She squeezed her eyes shut, sensing he was about to explode.

He stood and tipped his chair on the floor. "What? Don't tell me that and expect me not to be concerned or angry, Katy. What were you thinking? Putting your life in danger like that when you have a family..."

Katy smiled and tugged on his arm. "Sit down, stop mouthing off and listen to me."

He righted his chair and sat again. She reached for both of his hands and held them tight as she relayed the events of the day.

"Jesus. Why? Why put yourself in danger like that? Why not call for the armed response guys right away? I can't figure out if you're brave or stupid."

"Thanks, I'm gravitating more towards being brave myself."

"Why didn't you come straight home from the hospital? I'll be having words with Charlie about this."

"Oh no you won't. She insisted I come home, but I was determined to work on. My head got clearer by the hour. Yes, it's a bit muzzy now, but that's to be expected."

"Because I'm having a go at you, that's what you're saying, right?"

She grinned. "Possibly. AJ, look at it this way, I'm still here. Living and breathing and sitting right here with my gorgeous, caring fella. Now, answer my question, where's Georgie?"

"She's staying at a friend's house, it was a last-minute decision. I was kind of put on the spot when Samir asked me at the school gate in front of Georgie. I didn't have the heart to say no, her eyes were silently pleading with me."

"Aw...I know how persuasive she can be. She's got us both wrapped around her little finger, hasn't she? Hey, all turned out good in the end, saved you dragging her to the party, didn't it?"

"That's not why I did it. But yes, it worked out well for both of us."

"And how did your first gig go down?"

"Brilliantly." His face lit up, all the worry lines dispersing in an instant.

Katy's heart warmed. "I'm so pleased. Tell me all about it. I'm dying to know all the details."

He glanced over at the stove. "Let me finish off the dinner first. I need to put the pasta on."

"Have I got time to get changed?"

"Sure. Do you need me to help you get up the stairs?"

Katy tutted and shook her head. "Nope, but thanks for caring."

They shared a kiss, and both smiled when they parted.

"I wouldn't be the same if ever I lost you, Katy."

"Ditto, sweet cheeks." She rose from her chair and clutched the side of the table to keep herself upright for an instant. Luckily, AJ was none the wiser because he was already pouring the pasta into the pot and filling it with water from the kettle. "I won't be long."

AJ was too busy concentrating on his creation to notice her leave. She held on tight to the bannister and made it up the stairs without further incident. After entering the bedroom, she sank onto the comfy mattress, removed her jacket and undid her blouse. Hitching it off her shoulders produced a sharp pain that pulled at her chest. She stood and surveyed the damage the butt of the killer's gun had caused. Above her breasts lay an angry bruise the size of a clenched boxing glove. She winced and traced the bruise with her fingertips. *Fucker, you really did a number on me. One way or another, I'm going to make you pay for hurting me, mark my words!*

After having a quick wash, instead of changing into her leisure suit, she decided to slip into a pair of heavyweight tartan pyjamas, ones that had a zipper at the neck which she knew would hide the damage from AJ.

She eased her way back down the stairs and into the kitchen.

AJ turned her way. "That's unusual for you to get ready for bed so early. Are you sure you're okay?"

"I'm fine. Being lazy and cutting out a chore for later, that's all. Is dinner ready yet? Want me to lay the table?"

"Nope, it's all in hand. I thought we'd be slouches tonight and have it on our laps in front of the TV, if that's okay with you?"

She smiled. "What you're really saying is you intend to make the most of not running around after a five-year-old."

"That as well. Go through, I'm going to dish up. There's a list of films I've noted down on the pad in there. Take your pick, and we can start watching it as soon as I bring the dinner in."

"I wouldn't know where to begin, the choice is yours tonight."

"I'll sort it out then. Fancy a glass of wine? Will your head take it?"

"I'm not sure. I think I'll stick with an orange juice, if that's all right?"

"Of course it is."

Dinner turned out to be the satisfaction her body was craving to ease her pain and discomfort. Engrossed in the film, AJ cuddled her, and she drifted off to sleep not long after she'd devoured her spaghetti bolognaise. She woke up a few hours later when AJ tried to lift her from the couch. "Leave me here, I'll be fine," she mumbled sleepily.

So he did.

5

$\mathcal{K}$aty drove into work, her head still groggy from the decent night's sleep she'd had. AJ fussed around, fixing her a cooked breakfast which she gobbled down after her morning shower. She'd studied the bruising to her forehead and chest in the steamed-up mirror. They were both far more prominent than the night before. She'd ensured she got changed in the bathroom that morning, in case AJ noticed the discolouration to her chest.

Arriving at the station, she was delighted to find the rest of the team already seated at their desks. She smiled, trying to convince them she felt perkier than she actually did, knowing that a couple of coffees would brighten her mood within the first hour.

Katy carried her first caffeine fix into the office. The phone rang within seconds of her taking a seat. Coffee in hand, she answered the call and then took a welcoming sip.

"Sorry to trouble you, ma'am…"

"Go on, Mick, it's always ominous when you ring me."

"I've heard something along the lines that there's been a shooting, ma'am, and thought I'd give you the heads-up first, before anyone else."

"Shit! What type of shooting?"

"One involving bullets. Sorry, I couldn't resist it. I'm not sure if it's connected to what went on yesterday, but I'd rather highlight it from the outset. Wouldn't want you coming down heavily on me if it turns out I screwed up."

"You're a very wise man. I'll make the team aware and be with you in a few minutes. Have the details ready for me."

"Will do, ma'am."

Katy slurped at her drink, annoyed it wasn't cool enough for her to finish it. She detested taking drinks in the car with her. The idea always turned out to be a bad one when it went cold before she remembered to drink it.

She entered the incident room. "Charlie, sup up, we're on the move. I've had word of another shooting. Unsure if it's connected to the investigation as yet. We'll know more once we've attended the scene. I need you guys to make a start on obtaining all the CCTV footage and sifting through the backgrounds of the victims, in our absence, and don't forget to seek help from your contacts on the street."

She and Charlie made their way out of the station.

She threw Charlie the keys to her car. "You can drive, I'm still not a hundred percent, and that's between you and me. I don't want it going any further, you hear me?"

"I do. I'll bite down on the lecture that's sitting on the tip of my tongue then. It wouldn't do any good airing it anyway, would it?"

Katy smiled over the top of her car. "You're learning quickly, partner."

Charlie shook her head and got in. The journey was easier with the aid of the siren. Fifteen minutes later, Charlie brought the car to a halt outside a three-storey townhouse, the render of which had been painted in a deep pink.

"Yuck, who would want to do that to their house?"

"Maybe they inherited the colour. Either that or their intent was to make a statement, and they've definitely succeeded there."

There was a huge police presence. SOCO and Patti were in attendance and in the process of setting up.

"I have a couple of spare suits in the boot. I'll get them," Katy announced. She hung on to the door and eased herself out.

"Shit, boss. You can't work in that state," Charlie reprimanded her through a hissed exchange.

"Hush now. I'll be fine in a moment. It passes within seconds, once I'm upright."

"There's no point in me saying anything, is there?" Charlie joined her at the rear of the car, and the boot sprang open.

"Nope. Give it a rest, partner. I'm fine. The more you go on about it the more I'll dig my heels in."

"You don't say." Charlie extracted a suit and stepped into it.

Katy could tell Charlie was narked. Neither of them spoke again until they reached Patti.

"Hello, you two. Hard to tell if this is connected or not. I thought I'd jump in early before you got around to asking the inevitable question. How's your head? It looks nasty."

Katy inhaled a breath. "It's getting better by the hour, stop fussing. I can't catch a bloody killer sitting on my sofa at home, can I? Now, I know you both mean well." She pointed at Patti and then Charlie. "But the quicker you realise I'm not about to give in to this the better. Back to the reason why we're here, if you don't mind?"

Patti pulled a face at her. "Pardon me for caring. I won't bother in the future."

"Patti! I didn't mean to offend. You'd be the same if the tables were turned, and don't try and tell me otherwise."

"Okay, you might have a point there. Let's call it a truce for now. What have we got here? Well, our victim was arriving home from his shift at a factory—he works nights, and no, he hasn't been here all night before you leap on me for that."

Katy smiled. "The thought hadn't occurred to me to ask. Go on."

"He parked the car, and a couple of the neighbours said a man emerged from the hedge and opened fire on him. Just gunned him down in broad daylight without a frigging care in the world."

"Don't tell me, the gunman was wearing a damn mask?"

"You've got it. His disguise is giving him untold bravery, that's what I'm reading into it."

"Yep, I'm inclined to agree with you. The witnesses, did they say anything else?"

"No, I called a halt to that. I've got enough on my plate with three victims to cut open and analyse. It's your job to get to the nitty-gritty side of things."

Katy stared at her. "Are you taking the piss? I'm well aware of what our job entails, I don't need to be reminded by you or anyone else."

Patti stared at Katy and then turned her attention to Charlie. "My advice would be to get your partner out of my face if she's going to take that tone with me."

Charlie shuffled her feet, seemingly uncomfortable to be stuck in the middle.

Patti and Katy burst out laughing.

"Had you worried there, Charlie," Patti said. "You'll get used to us sniping at each other, we're the best of friends deep down."

Charlie's head swivelled between Katy and Patti. "Thanks, guys. I nearly shat myself back there, then."

"On with the case," Katy said. It felt good to feel normal again after a rough twelve hours or so. "Charlie, I need you to question the witnesses. Take down any relevant information from them but leave a statement for now, we haven't got the time. I'll ask uniform to sort that out later."

Patti pointed at a cluster of people off to the left. "They're over there. Good luck."

"Thanks," Charlie said and walked off.

Katy smiled at Patti. "We're going to have to stop doing that, her face was a picture."

"Yeah, we should. Right, professional heads on." Patti took a few steps towards the body which had been covered with a white sheet.

Katy crouched down beside her, and her knee dropped to the ground.

"Are you all right?" Patti asked.

"I'm fine. Sudden movements tend to catch me off-guard, that's all. How many times was he shot?"

"At least six. All to the chest. There was no way he could survive such an ambush."

"What a shame. Do we know who he is?"

"His significant other is inside, you'll need to speak to her. When we arrived, she wasn't making much sense."

"Bugger, poor woman. I'll nip in and see her soon. Was the killer hanging around, aware of what time he got home? Or did he follow him home and make a concerted effort to kill him outside his house?"

"I can't give you an answer to either of those, sorry, not in my remit."

"I know. Just me thinking out loud. I'll see what the wife has to say and speak to you later."

Katy glanced over her shoulder at Charlie who was busy scribbling down some notes while the three men animatedly spoke to her. *I'd still rather swap roles with her at the moment.*

Sucking in a few calming breaths, she rang the bell and waited for the woman to answer. She didn't have to wait long. "Hi, I'm the Senior Investigating Officer, DI Katy Foster. Can I come in and have a chat with you? Are you up to it?"

The young blonde wiped away the tears and dabbed a tissue under her nose. "Yes, come in."

Katy followed her into a cosy lounge, a gas fire ablaze on high, obviously to combat the shock she was suffering. The woman sat and clenched her hands tightly in her lap.

Katy noticed them trembling.

"Why?" the woman whispered without looking up.

"I don't know is the truthful answer. I was hoping you would be able to point us in the right direction."

"Me? I know nothing. We were so happy, content and planning our wedding. Oh God, that's never going to happen now, is it? Of course it isn't, not if he's dead." She shook her head and swiped at the fresh tears falling.

"You have my sincere condolences. I can imagine how difficult this must be for you right now. Are you up to talking to me? Is there anyone I can call to come and be with you?"

"No. I can deal with this by myself—at least I think I can. Why him? He's done nothing wrong. He gets on with everyone and enjoys his job. Who would do such a thing?"

"Have you known each other long?"

"Around three years."

"Where did you meet?"

Her face lit up. "I was on a night out with my girlfriends. He asked me to slow dance with him at the end of the evening, and I lost my heart to him that night." She sobbed and covered her face with her shaking hands.

"I'm so sorry, I know this is hard for you. Please, had your fiancé recently fallen out with anyone perhaps?"

"No, as I said, we were making plans to get married. He hasn't seen his friends in months; we've been tied up every night, going through all the arrangements."

"What about at work? Has he had a possible run-in with anyone there, perhaps?"

"No, they think the world of him there. He was the night manager on the shift. People came to him if they had any problems or were in trouble of any kind. Oh God…" She glanced at the door and shook her head. "I can't believe he's never going to walk through that door again, ever. How will I cope without him? We had become inseparable since we announced our wedding a few months ago. Everyone was so happy for us." She motioned at the cards decorating the pieces of furniture as well as the two windowsills.

"It would help if you could give me some background information on your fiancé, sorry, what was his name? I should have asked."

"Rufus Wright."

"And yours is?"

"Camilla Boyd."

"May I call you Camilla?"

"Of course. I can't give you anything else, my mind is in turmoil at the moment. I can't think beyond seeing him lying there out on the pavement. Am I ever going to be able to rid myself of the images? If so, when? Every time I close my eyes, I see him. His eyes wide open, staring at me but unable to see me. He'll never know how much I loved him. How much I will grieve for him. I will never meet someone as caring as he was, ever."

"What about past girlfriends, did he have many of those?"

She swallowed and nodded. "Back in the day he had an eye for the ladies, but when we met, everything changed. That night we fell in love and…"

"I understand. Over the last few months, do you recall Rufus having any dealings with any of his exes?"

"No, nothing. He would have told me. We had no secrets."

"What about you? Have you had many previous boyfriends?"

"Years ago, before I met my fiancé."

"Ah, you've been married before."

Her cheeks flared up. "I was married when I met Rufus. I went home that night and told my husband our marriage was over."

"After one dance with Rufus you were prepared to go to such lengths?"

"That's how deeply we fell in love."

"I can't imagine your husband being too impressed when he heard the news."

She shrugged. "There was nothing he could do to change my mind. I moved out within a few days and came here to live with Rufus. My husband accepted it, sort of."

"I need to tell you that I'm already running an investigation into two other murders in the area. We believe there is a possible link."

She gasped. "No. Really?"

Katy nodded. "Did your fiancé know either a Grace Hunt or Colin Markham?"

Her eyes widened. "I'm not sure if he knew them but I've heard their names." Her brow knitted together.

"May I ask how you know them?"

"Through my ex."

Katy withdrew her notebook and pen. "And his name would be?"

74

"James Boyd."

"And how would your ex have known Grace and Colin?"

"Through his job at Zedex."

Katy raised her head swiftly, cricking her neck in the process. "Sorry? He works at Zedex?"

"Yes, at least I think he still does. Maybe I'm wrong about that. I haven't been in touch with him in a while."

"How long has it been since you last saw him?"

"A few weeks ago. Rufus and I went round there to see him. He's been stubborn about signing the divorce papers. We implored him to get on with it as our wedding has been booked and was due to take place in a few months. Yet another job that we wanted to tick off our huge list."

"I see, and what was his response?"

"He was angry. I've never seen him flare up like that before. I urged Rufus to get back in the car. He refused to leave me alone with James as he felt my ex was unstable."

"Interesting. Can I have James's address?"

"It's sixty-seven Todmarsh Road. Please don't tell me he's the one responsible for this?"

"I can't answer that right now. He's definitely a person of interest as there is a possible link to all three crimes."

"Oh God. I hope you're wrong. If you're not, then I'm going to carry a burden of guilt with me for the rest of my days. How dreadful. When you think you know someone and they turn out to be a killer."

Katy raised a hand. "Let's not get carried away with that theory just yet. I'll need to have a word with him to determine what he knows about the events which have taken place over the past twenty-four hours. One thing, did your ex own a gun?"

"I don't think so. Not while I was with him anyway."

"May I ask how long you two were together?"

"Over ten years."

"And up until you met Rufus on a night out you were happy together?"

Camilla stared off at the wall to her left. "I suppose the warning signs were there at the beginning, but I was in love and pushed them aside, chose to ignore them."

"Warning signs? How did they manifest themselves?"

"He liked to control me. Told me who I could see and what I should wear. I suppose I rebelled and that's why I was out with my friends that night."

"How did you manage to get away from him for the evening?"

"I had to make out I was going on a course relating to work. He fell for it, I stayed at a friend's house. A few of my other girlfriends joined us. They worked on me, you know, dressed me up, had a go at me for being dowdy and getting old before my time, and the rest was history. The next thing I knew, they were dragging me out for a night on the town. I got tipsy early on and sat alone for a while until they forced me to get up on the dance floor. One of the girls pointed out Rufus to me. She told me he'd had his eye on me for over an hour. I turned all giggly; it had been a while since any man had shown me any kind of attention. He was such a sweetheart. I became aware of his reputation; he didn't hold back but he told me I was the one he'd been waiting to spend the rest of his life with. And now…he's gone."

Katy sighed. "Life is so tough at times. And James accepted it when you chose to leave him? Or did he kick up a fuss?" *Katy asked a second time, needing to clarify things.*

"No, he accepted it, even told me he was in the wrong for neglecting me over the years. I appreciated his honesty, and Rufus and I decided to move on with our lives and never to discuss him again, until the day came when we received notice from the solicitors that James was digging his heels in about signing the divorce papers. We told our solicitor we'd pay him a visit. She advised us against doing that, but we did it anyway."

"And what kind of reception did you get?"

"I'd worked myself up into a frenzy. He opened the door. At first, he was angry to see us standing there together but accepted things for what they were and invited us in. He apologised and said work had been manic for several weeks and all he was guilty of doing was coming home at night and flaking out on the sofa. From what I could recall, he used to do that a lot every time work put too much pressure on him."

"What was his role at Zedex?"

"He worked closely with Grace Hunt. I've got it somewhere in the back of my mind that he told us she might have grabbed the promotion that was due to him, but you'll need to check I've got that right."

"What's his background? Any episodes of unstable mental health over the years?"

"No, nothing that I'm aware of. As I said earlier, he liked to control me. Maybe that's an indication that things weren't that good in his early life."

"What about his parents?"

"They're both dead. His mother died when he was a mere babe in arms, and his father was forced to bring him up on his own."

"You're telling me there was no female influence in his life from a very young age?"

"I suppose I am. Do you think that's contributed to him being unstable?" She shuddered. "Oh God, to think I lived with the man, laid down beside him every night for almost ten years. Had sex with him, and all the time…"

"Try not to put yourself through the mental torture of thinking about that."

"But if you're telling me that he's gone on a killing spree, shit, do you think I'm next?"

Katy shrugged. "Don't worry. It might not be him. We'll take every precaution to keep you safe. I'll organise a safe house for you if necessary. My advice would be to pack a suitcase after we finish speaking, just to be on the safe side, in case the killer returns. I can make the arrangements while you do that."

"Thank you so much. Shall I do it now?"

"Yes, I'll call the station, make the arrangements. It could take a few hours to sort out for you. You're safe, we won't leave you alone."

Camilla rushed out of the room, and Katy took her phone from her pocket. She rang her contact in witness protection to seek their advice first. They told her they had a property available and would arrange to pick Camilla up to take her there. Katy said that wasn't necessary and that she would personally drop Camilla off at the station just in case the killer was hanging around and followed them out to the house. Her contact agreed. After ending the call, Katy rang the incident room to speak to Karen. She gave her colleague a brief rundown on what had gone on and asked her to carry out all the necessary checks needed on James Boyd.

Katy then went outside to see what Charlie had discovered, if anything. She placed a uniformed officer at the door and issued instructions for him not to let anyone else into the house, except for the professionals dealing with the case.

Charlie saw her, excused herself from the gentlemen she was talking to and headed towards Katy. "Any good?"

Charlie nodded. "Sort of. A lot of waffle and possible conspiracy theories flying around which I had to sift through. Maybe you can take a look at what I've written down and tell me if I did the right thing in discounting certain information."

"Bollocks, will I. I trust you. Give me a brief recap, and I'll tell you what I've learnt from the victim's significant other."

"Sounds ominous. I bet your fishing trip was more lucrative than mine. One of the guys, no, make that two of them, said the killer pulled up in a blue Honda. They couldn't give me an exact model, but I do have a partial number plate to be going on with."

"Excellent news. Go on."

Charlie flipped open her notebook. "They told me the driver drew up in a hurry, got out of the vehicle, took shelter behind a hedge, and then, in front of the three men, without a care in the world, he opened fire on the victim. The men took off, fearing for their lives. One of them said the killer shot at him, but the other two said he was mistaken. They admitted they couldn't really tell because they were that intent on running away from the scene they didn't bother looking back until the killer drove off."

"I see. Anything else?"

"A lot of projective possible suggestions as to who the masked, oops, I forgot to tell you that bit, yes, it would appear our masked man was the culprit."

"Okay. First of all, get in touch with base. Tell them what you've got on the car and get a couple of members of the team searching the ANPRs in the area, focusing around the time the incident occurred."

Charlie nodded and stepped away. In the meantime, Katy walked over to have a brief chat with Patti.

"How's it going?" she asked, glancing down at the body.

"I'm almost ready to shift him back to the mortuary. SOCO will hang around though. How are things at your end?"

"I've got the name of a possible suspect. He had a motive for each of the crimes, and yes, they're related, that much is certain."

"Do tell, don't keep me in suspenders." Patti smiled.

"Rather than repeat myself, can I wait until Charlie gets here? She's getting the team to run a potential car and plate for the killer."

"Rightio! It all sounds promising."

Charlie joined them. "All actioned. Let's hope we get something from it. Are you going to tell me what the victim's other half said?"

"From speaking with her, I have no doubt in my mind who our prime suspect is."

"Who?" Patti and Charlie said in unison.

"The woman's estranged husband, James Boyd. We'll need to corroborate which car he drives."

"I doubt if he would use his own car, it'll probably be stolen," Charlie suggested.

"Okay, good point. If true, that will hamper our investigation further still. Get this, he works for Zedex, still does as far as she knows. We need to check into it. She mentioned about Grace getting promoted which I thought was odd."

"Whoa! Seriously, was he overlooked for the promotion?"

"Possibly. Camilla is his soon-to-be ex-wife. They were waiting for the divorce to come through before they could get hitched. She and the victim, Rufus Wright, visited James a few weeks ago. I'm thinking either the promotion or the visit from his ex to do with the divorce, was the trigger that initiated the murders."

Patti nodded slowly. "Sounds like a plausible assumption to me. Does he own a gun?"

"The wife didn't seem to think so, but hey, with the right contacts and money to burn in his pocket, guns are easily sought on the black market, right? The guys back at the station are following up on that front now."

"That's true," Charlie agreed. "What about Camilla? She won't be safe here, will she?"

"No, my sentiments exactly. I've told her to pack a bag. We'll take her back to the station and hand her over to the witness protection guys. I've already sounded them out and arranged possible accommodation for her."

"I bet she's devastated. Any clues on what his character was like during their marriage?" Charlie asked.

"He was a controller. She had to make up an excuse about going on a course at work just so she could go out with her friends."

"At least her friends stuck by her. So many don't in similar circumstances," Patti replied.

"True enough. Anyway, that's where she met Rufus, on this said night out."

"Okay, and one thing led to another and she ended up leaving hubby, yes?" Charlie asked.

"Yep, spot on. She moved in here with him, despite Rufus being a bit of a lad with the lasses. She told me he changed instantly once they hooked up. She was the one he'd been searching for, apparently."

"How romantic." Patti pretended to stick her fingers down her throat.

Katy slapped her arm. "Stop mocking, these things happen, to those who believe."

"Yeah, I'm glad I'm not one of them. Sad that he's dead all the same. I shouldn't mock. My mistake, sorry, ladies."

Katy smiled and rubbed her arm. "You're forgiven. Okay, we're going to leave you to it, Patti, and see if Camilla is ready to make a move."

Katy and Charlie entered the house.

There was no sign of Camilla downstairs, so Katy called out to her. "Camilla, how are things going up there?"

The house remained quiet.

Katy opened the front door and spoke to the officer on guard. "Has the lady of the house come out at all?"

"No, I haven't moved from this spot."

Katy and Charlie charged up the stairs. They split up at the top, searching each of the rooms off the large landing.

"Charlie, in here."

Lying in the bath of steaming hot water was a fully clothed Camilla. Her wrists were cut to ribbons, and there was an old-fashioned-type wet razor on the floor beside the bath.

"Ring for an ambulance, Charlie. Oh shit! Not on my watch, please."

Charlie exited the room and made the urgent call. She rejoined Katy and shared the news. "They're going to be at least ten minutes."

Katy's head was swimming. "I can't do this. You're going to have to take over, Charlie. I've checked her pulse, there's a faint one. We need to get her out of the bath."

"I'm off now, ladies. I'll be in touch soon," Patti shouted from downstairs.

"No, Patti. Up here in the bathroom, you've got to help us."

Patti's footsteps bounded up the stairs, and she instantly swooped in and brushed Katy and Charlie aside. "Let me get to her. Have you rung for an ambulance?"

"Yes. There's a faint pulse. Do your best for her, Patti."

"Goes without saying. Help me get her out of the bath."

The three of them struggled to lift the woman. Katy's strength wasn't up to much. She was relying on Charlie and Patti to do most of the heavy lifting. They placed her on the floor, and Patti set up about removing Camilla's clothes while Charlie tied a couple of small towels around her wrists to stop the bleeding.

"Go into the bedroom, get me her nightie or pyjamas and a dressing gown. Once she's undressed, we're going to need to dry her, have those on standby. While she has a pulse, I can't perform CPR on her,

81

it's more than I dare do. I'll monitor her in the meantime until the paramedics arrive," Patti said.

"Is it worth trying to bring her round?" Katy asked, her knees shaking, hampering her ability to stand upright.

"Katy, go and sit down before you sodding well fall down," Patti ordered.

Charlie returned with Camilla's PJs and placed them on the toilet seat and then proceeded to help Patti disrobe the woman.

Katy watched on from the doorway. "We can't let her die. Do something, Patti."

Patti lifted her head and glared at her. "Are you still here? I'm doing my best, give me a break. I'm used to dealing with stiffs, not live patients, remember."

"That's my concern." Katy grinned in an effort to ease the tension.

Patti shook her head and then breathed out a huge sigh. "I can hear the ambulance coming, what a relief. Hurry, Charlie, let's get her dried off and changed."

Camilla groaned softly.

"She's coming around," Katy said in a whisper.

"Camilla, can you hear me?" Patti asked, giving Camilla's shoulder a slight shake.

Another groan, and her eyes flickered open. "What? Where?" were the only two words the dazed young woman could manage before she burst into tears. "Why did you have to save me? Why? I want to be with Rufus. Let me go...I'm begging you, just let me go."

"We can't do that, love. I'm sorry, we'll get you the help you need. Hang in there," Katy replied. Never had she felt such sympathy for a woman as she did right then.

Two paramedics, both men in their early thirties, thundered up the stairs. Charlie and Patti joined Katy in the hallway, giving the men room in the small bathroom to assist Camilla. Then one of the paramedics ran down the stairs again and brought in a stretcher which he assembled under Katy's gaze.

She tapped the man on the shoulder and mouthed, "Is she going to be all right?"

He nodded. "She's going to be fine, we'll see to that."

"Thank you. We'll follow you, if that's okay?"

"That's up to you. My guess is that she'll possibly be sedated at the other end once the doctor has checked her over. It might be wise to leave her alone for twenty-four hours."

"Okay, I'll do that. Which hospital?"

"St Thomas'."

The two men eased Camilla onto the stretcher and carried her downstairs and into the vehicle.

Katy jumped in the back for a final word with her. "Stay strong, Camilla. We'll get you through this."

"No one will be able to get me through this…only Rufus could do that, and he's no longer with us. I want to be with him. I belong with him."

"I'll drop by and see you tomorrow. Check how you're doing, I promise."

"No. I'd rather you stay away. You should be out there, searching for him. He's done this, he needs to be fucking punished. I don't want to see you again unless it's to tell me that you've caught the bastard, you hear me?"

"Don't worry. We'll catch whoever is responsible for the crimes."

"It's him. James! Why can't you see that?"

"Yes, he's our main suspect. All the evidence we've gathered so far is leading us to believe it's him, but there could be something far more sinister afoot here. It could be possible that someone is setting him up, have you thought about that?"

"I don't believe it. Just get out there and find him. I need justice for Rufus, my darling Rufus."

"And you'll get it. I promise you will."

6

*H*e watched from behind a neighbour's hedge. An alley ran up the side of the house, he could use that to escape if someone spotted him, but they wouldn't. He was better than that. Well-practised at the art of deceit—he'd had to be over the years.

Fear struck his heart. He'd heard the ambulance arrive and he'd thought Rufus had survived. He should have known that wasn't the case, not with the pathologist and SOCO at the scene. Why had they run into the house? He'd been tempted to move closer for a better look but decided it would be far wiser for him to remain where he was, peering through the hole he'd made in the hedge to create a perfect viewing slot.

When the stretcher emerged, carrying his beloved Camilla, he almost blew his cover. What was wrong with her? She looked dreadful, pale and gaunt. Had she been eating well? He'd always ensured she ate plenty when she was at home with him.

We did good, two birds with one stone!

"What are you talking about?"

We killed him and nearly got rid of her as well. You should be pleased. She left you, dimwit, or are you forgetting that?

"No, no, how could I ever forget that? You're to blame, you did this. There was no 'we' about it."

Bollocks! It was your finger on the trigger. You're the guilty party. I just goaded you into making the move. Gave you the balls needed to retaliate, that's all. You need to grow a pair of your own, man. The sooner the better. Our job has only just begun.

"I'm not sure I want to continue. All this is your doing, not mine. You forced me into this. I was quite happy plodding along. Yes, I'd lost my soul mate, but I would've survived eventually."

Yeah, yeah, of course you would! You said that after she died. And yet you let that fuckwit treat you like shit in your formative years.

"Leave them out of it. I'm over that. Past it. I don't want to revisit what went on back then. I can't do anything about that. It's the future I need to consider now, not live in the vile past. He moulded me. I regard myself as a decent person."

Don't be so absurd. You, decent? After the murders you've committed in the last few days.

Laughter rang out in his head.

"You're guilty of that. Not me. I had nothing to do with those murders."

Hogwash, you don't know what you're bloody saying half the time. That bastard beat every ounce of common sense out of you at such a young age.

"He made me stronger, more resilient. I was coping just fine until you popped up. Your nagging and vitriol are relentless. I wish you'd do one and bugger off. Leave me to live my life in peace. Now that Rufus is no longer around, I know she'll come running back to be in my arms again."

Ha! And you think I'm the delusional one. Get a grip, man! She ain't coming back, and who could blame her?

"Shut up, just shut the fuck up. She will, I have every faith in our love. She'll soon come to realise I'm the only man who ever treated her right."

Are you for real? She's on her way to hospital after trying to kill herself because you just killed her one true love. I can't make it any clearer for you, and you're still not grasping it, are you?

"Shut up. She's mine. She'll be back in my bed soon enough, now he's no longer around to tempt her away from me."

Whatever! It's your call at the end of the day. Are we going to stick around here for long?

"Why the rush? It's not like you have anything planned."

That shut the bastard up. During his internal conversation, his attention had remained on the female detective who appeared to be in charge of the investigation, and he wondered if she had it in her to figure it all out and to capture him.

Only time would tell.

He watched until the ambulance drove past, taking the love of his life with it.

7

"*R*ight, we've got a new lead to follow up on finally, peeps," Katy began after she'd called the team together back in the incident room. "We need to find out all there is to know about James Boyd. There's a possibility he's our killer, according to his estranged wife, who also happens to be this victim's fiancée." She pointed at the third victim; she brought the whiteboard up to date as she slotted the pieces together.

"Want me to make a start while you continue, boss?" Karen asked.

"If you would. Our suspect works at Zedex, according to his soon to be ex-wife. We need to find out the facts. At present he appears to be the only possible link between the victims. Unfortunately, Camilla is currently in hospital after attempting to take her own life. If Charlie, Patti and I hadn't been there...well, I doubt if she'd still be with us. Distressing when a loved one is gunned down because of your involvement with the killer. I fear that's what was behind her trying to end her life. I wouldn't want to be in her shoes. I promised her we'd find him, and that's exactly what I intend to do. No matter what costs are involved. He's up in the realms of serial killer already, and that after what, a total of thirty-six hours? Let's get this shithead caught, and swiftly, guys."

A loud roar went up in response, and a couple of the men thundered their hands on their desks.

"All right, calm down. Let's make every second count on this one. Each of you knows what you have to do. I know you won't let me down."

"Are we going to go see James?" Charlie called over from the vending machine.

"I'm undecided on that one. I'm going to see the chief, see what he thinks we should do. You might as well all know, there's a letter sitting on my desk, telling me that funding is tight and warning about wasting money unnecessarily. I need to get clarification from the boss what that means exactly. I'll be back soon. Crack on in the meantime."

Katy left the incident room and marched up the long hallway to DCI Roberts' office.

"Hello, Inspector. Is he expecting you?" Trisha asked. "Ouch! That looks nasty."

"It is. I'm fine, though. I was hoping you could squeeze me in. I wouldn't ask if I didn't think it was important."

"Leave it with me, I'll have a word in his shell-like."

Trisha knocked on the chief's door. He bellowed in response, and she disappeared inside. She emerged a few seconds later and held the door open for Katy to enter.

"He can spare you five minutes, just enough time for a nice cup of coffee, eh?"

"Don't bother, she won't have the time to drink it," Roberts shouted before Katy could even open her mouth.

She rolled her eyes at Trisha. "Thanks for the offer anyway."

Trisha smiled awkwardly and closed the door behind Katy.

She tentatively took a few steps closer to Roberts' desk. "I can come back later if you can't spare the time right now. It's no biggie."

"Sit down, Inspector. What do you want to bend my ear about this time?" He looked up, and his eyes widened. "Where the fuck did you get that?"

"I'm fine. A confrontation with the killer, that's all. Getting back to what you said, bend your ear? Not sure I've ever done that. Right, first of all, I want to get clarification on the new budget slashes. Does that include me and my team?"

"Of course it does, why shouldn't it?"

"Because it takes a lot of time to solve murders, and I'm getting the impression that someone is directly having a go at me."

"Stop with the woe is me, I used to get enough of that with your predecessor. You shouldn't take things to heart. We're all in the same boat. We've just got to deal with it and make the most of the funds we have at our disposal."

"Okay. Can I also say that I don't appreciate being compared to my predecessor? I'm not saying I had anything against Lorne, you know that. But stop flinging it at me every time I raise a subject or do something which isn't to your liking."

He sat back and steepled his fingers, a smirk pulling at his lips. "Okay, guilty as charged. I wondered how long it would take you to have the balls to shoot me down."

"What? You were bloody testing me?" She rubbed at her forehead, consciously avoiding the bruise.

"I do that occasionally. Now, what can I help you with? What's going on with the investigation? And how come you let the killer slip through your fingers?"

Katy groaned and then disclosed everything they had up until now, delivering it without taking a breath.

"I see. I take it you're going to arrest this James Boyd then?"

"Should we? Or should we keep him under surveillance for a few days?"

"Why the dilemma and if he's killed so quickly already, who's to say he won't continue his spree today?"

"Because all we have is hearsay that it could be him. Yes, there are several motives, but you know what CPS is like, if there is no DNA or evidence to back up the claims, we're thigh high in shit."

He nodded. "I get that. Didn't you get a look at him when he knocked seven bells out of you?"

"No. He was wearing a mask."

"Unfortunate. Okay, then I agree with you, put the man under surveillance for the next two days."

Katy chewed her lip.

"What's wrong now?"

"We have to locate the bugger first. My guess is that he'll go on the run."

Roberts expelled a frustrated sigh. "Who's toying with whom here?"

Katy sniggered. "Two people can play your game, sir. No, in all honesty, it's true, we've yet to locate him. His estranged wife tried to commit suicide before I could ask if she knew where he could be now."

"Is she all right? Do you think she'll try it again?"

"Who knows? It depends on her mental state. My take is that she might—her self-worth is at a possible all-time low at present."

"In that case, she's in the best place for her."

"She can't stay in hospital indefinitely, though, and when she comes out that responsibility is down to me. I've arranged to put her in a safe house, but she'll be alone at the residence, who's to say she won't try it again the minute she's left alone?"

"I hear you. Maybe if she feels bad enough, she'll reconsider trying to take her life a second time."

"I hope so. We'll deal with that should it crop up in the future. You're telling me if we track this bastard down that I can throw some funds at the investigation?"

"Yes, within reason."

"I have to justify my decisions, in other words."

"Yes, we all do. Stop taking this as a personal slight against you and your team. The directive went out to every high-ranking officer in the force from inspectors upwards."

"That's reassuring. It doesn't alter things, though. There's a serial killer on the loose around here, and instead of giving the case my full and undivided attention, I have to pause and think whether the expenditure that accompanies an investigation of this magnitude is justified or not. Makes you wonder how Head Office expect us to solve any crimes at all, doesn't it? What a deplorable position to be in."

"Hey, I'm with you all the way with that perspective. It is what it is, and we need to adapt or…"

"Or?"

"Let's hope it doesn't come to that. On that note, I need to crack on. Just be cautious, I'd go as far as telling you to be restrained in your approach on this case."

"Restrained? As in, every facet of the investigation or only the financial side of things?" Katy asked. She could tell Sean had picked up on the sarcasm laced throughout the question from the narrowing of his eyes.

"Be very careful, DI Foster."

Katy placed an innocent hand on her chest. "Oh, don't worry, I will." She rose from her chair, walked towards the door, yanked it open and threw over her shoulder, "And the concussion is passable today, but I'll plod on. Ever the professional, sir."

His mouth dropped open and tried to close a few times, but some kind of force appeared to be preventing it.

Katy didn't hang around to hear the sharp-tongued retort she sensed would be coming her way once he'd had the chance to recover.

"Everything all right?" Trisha whispered conspiratorially.

"Yep. It is now." Katy giggled and left the outer office.

Back in the incident room, she announced, "Listen up, folks, we've got the initial go-ahead to start surveillance, but it has an added warning not to be wasteful of the funds in place."

The team all groaned.

Patrick threw his pen across the desk. "How do they expect us to do our jobs properly working under the current restrictions, boss?"

"I asked the same thing and have no doubt that, in the past, numerous inspectors before me have done the same. I'm not happy about it but, let's do the best we can under the restrictions."

"Is it always like this?" Charlie asked.

"More often than not. We're just like any other business out there, Charlie. Head Office has a balance sheet they need to tally up at the end of each financial year. We must be nearing the end of ours, hence the restrictive measures in place."

"Oh, I see. Do you think you should make a public announcement, pleading with the criminals in the area to give us a break for a few months until the new financial year kicks in then?"

Katy smiled. "Can you imagine the uproar that would bring? You'll get used to it. We've coped before and we'll cope again. I've always tried to keep the overtime down to a minimum, the chief knows that. But I had fun reminding him what a crack team we are and pointing out our stunning achievements along the way. The trouble is, it's not him we should be worried about. He's behind us all the way, I don't want you guys to think otherwise."

Applause sounded from the doorway, and Katy swivelled on her heel, the motion almost sending her off balance.

"I couldn't have put it better myself, Inspector," Roberts shouted, his gaze boring into hers.

"Sorry, sir, I didn't see you there."

"That much is evident. Glad you weren't too over the top in your damning assessment, Inspector."

She recapped her recent words, trying to think if she'd called him any vile names or spoken unkindly about him. She hadn't. Katy breathed out a sigh. "I was simply relaying the message you gave me, sir. I'd rather make that point clear first before we truly sink our teeth into this investigation."

Roberts entered the room and approached the whiteboard. He scanned the information and then turned to face the team who were all staring at him anxiously. "No need to look so nervous, guys. I know we're asking a lot of you, and some of you will need to adapt the way you do things, but it's the way it has to be. Either that, or we'll be forced to make drastic cutbacks, so you tell me which is the lesser of the two evils."

"We get that, sir. We're intelligent individuals, otherwise we wouldn't be here. It doesn't mean we have to like working under a microscope, though," Katy batted back.

"I'm not asking you to. All I said was be mindful of how you spend the budget. Now, run me through what you've got. Let's try and figure out whether there are alternative measures we can put in place that will make all our lives a lot easier to cope with."

"We're going to carry out the background checks on James Boyd. We've got his address. All we need now is to find out what he's been up to lately. We've also got a partial plate on a blue Honda we can be looking into."

"I'll do that, boss," Patrick volunteered.

"Thanks. Steven, will you stick with the CCTV and ANPRs around the area of today's murder?"

"I will."

"What about evidence found at the earlier scenes?" Roberts asked.

"I'll be chasing up Forensics later today. I think it's way too early for them to have anything for us just yet."

"Try. That's all we can do. How sure are you that James Boyd is our man?"

"Joining the dots, he has to be, although in the eyes of the CPS we haven't got enough to nail him. I'm aiming to change that status during the next twenty-four to forty-eight hours, providing we can track the man down. Why?"

Roberts appeared thoughtful for a second or two. "I was wondering if it might be worth running a press conference."

"Outing him? Before we've got anything else in place? Is that wise?"

Roberts shrugged. "It would be a means to an end."

"Personally, I think it would have a negative effect without gathering the background information for him first."

"Explain why," Roberts challenged her.

"Let's face it, although we have his address, I doubt he'll be there, and if he's not there we need to uncover other possible addresses where he's likely to be hiding. As for his alternative employment, we've yet to establish that. Until we obtain the basics, our hands are tied."

"In that case, I suggest you get on with things." Roberts smiled and marched out of the room.

Katy shook her head in his wake. "Logical, right?" She rolled her eyes and motioned for the team to crack on with their tasks. "I'll be in my office, eagerly anticipating your findings, guys." She stepped into her office and rang Forensics. She knew what the answer would be long before the phone connected.

"Sorry, nothing yet. We've got teams attending several crimes today."

"What you're telling me is that you're stretched too thinly as usual," Katy muttered, her disappointment clearly showing.

"Sorry, in a nutshell, yes," the woman technician replied. "Want me to have a word with Patti, maybe get your cases put on the priority list?"

"I think they're probably up the top already, so let's leave things as they are for now. The last thing I want to do is piss her off. Keep things as they are for now."

"As if I'm likely to do that. We'll get back to you soon, I promise."

"I appreciate your help. Thanks." She ended the call and rang home.

AJ answered within a few minutes. "Hey, is everything all right?"

"I'm fine, just needed to hear your voice. A pig of a day already, and I don't foresee it getting any better in the short or long term."

"Ugh…sounds ominous. Anything I can do to help?"

"Make me laugh, try to brighten my dull and dreary day."

"Oh heck. Hang on, I heard a really dreadful joke the other day. What was it now…? Ah yes. Did you hear about the racing snail who got rid of his shell?"

"No, can't say I have."

"Wait for it…he thought it would make him faster, but it just made him sluggish."

Katy held back a groan and laughed. "Oh my, I wish I hadn't asked now, that was truly awful."

"Awfully good, though, and dare I say it, it appeared to do what it was intended to do and made you laugh."

"It did that. I'm super appreciative. How are things there?"

"I wasn't sure if I should call you or not. I've rung the doctors about Georgie."

"What? Is she all right? Oh God, I feel terrible and selfish now, you should have mentioned it as soon as I called. Oh heck…what if…?"

"Katy. Take a bloody breath. She's fine. A slight temperature and a bit sniffly. Samir rang me this morning, concerned about her. I went to pick her up from her house and came straight home. The doctor told me to monitor Georgie and to take her up to the hospital if she gets any worse."

"No medication? Nothing like that?"

"Nope, junior paracetamol, if I think it's necessary. I don't think it is, she's up there at the moment, zonked out. I checked her a few minutes ago."

Katy let out an exasperated breath. "We've had it too good with her lately. The specialist warned us she could have a relapse. We should have kept a closer eye on her, not allowed her to sleep over at another child's house. No one can take care of her as well as we can."

"Stop that. It's a mild cold. Stop getting yourself all worked up."

"What? I can't help it. I should be there with her, comforting her like any normal mother."

"Now you're talking utter nonsense, and thanks for doubting my ability to cope in the process."

"Bugger, I didn't mean to do that. I would never cast aspersions about your ability to care for our daughter. You do an amazing job, but it's natural for me to kick myself and throw a guilt-ridden analogy into the mix when things go wrong."

"I know, but I wish you wouldn't, it's not doing anyone any good. She'll be fine, I'm sure."

"Go check on her now, while I'm on the phone."

He tutted, and the phone hit the table. In the distance, AJ's footsteps sounded on the stairs. She strained her ear, hoping to pick up on any other possible noises, and then his measured footsteps returned a few moments later.

"Well?" she asked impatiently.

"She's fine. Snuggled up with Bear, not a care in the world. I told you not to worry."

"Did you feel her forehead? Does she have a temperature?"

95

"Katy...she's fine. Leave it there. If anything changes, I'll get her to the hospital immediately, I promise you."

She blew out a breath. "Thanks. I'm in no way doubting your parenting skills, don't ever think that. It's me being a worrying ninny, that's all."

"You're entitled to be. Now back to work with you, you have a case to solve."

"He's a spree killer now. Three murders all linked to one man."

"You know who it is?"

"Yep, all we've got to do now is find him."

"That's the hardest part, you have my sympathy."

"Thanks. I'd better get on now. Promise me you'll call me if Georgie's condition deteriorates."

"I promise. Don't worry, she's fine with her old dad caring for her."

"That's not my concern, and you know it."

"I do. Some men might get a complex, but I'm fine, honestly."

They both laughed.

"Cheeky sod. I love you and appreciate all you do for us. Any calls regarding the business today?"

"Yep, an extra couple of bookings. Next month is shaping up to be good so far."

"I'm thrilled for you. You've worked so hard to pull it all together."

"I know. Thanks for being such a supportive wife."

"Get away with you. I've gotta fly. If all goes well today, we'll have a celebratory drink or two later."

"I'll put a bottle in the fridge to chill."

Katy ended the call with a smile on her face. It slipped soon after she placed the phone in the docking station. She couldn't bear it if anything happened to Georgie. Although, the consultant did say that they should prepare for things to get worse before they got any better. Why did God have to punish children in this way? If he was angry with the parents then take it out on them and not the innocent babies out there. Some of whom are born with a heart defect, such as Georgie. Where was the justice in that?

Charlie knocked on her door and poked her head into the room. "Everything okay? What's wrong, Katy?"

Katy brushed away the tear that had seeped onto her cheek. "Nothing, me being silly, that's all. What have you got?"

"We've confirmed James Boyd's address via the electoral roll."

Katy rubbed her hands together in glee, pushing aside her own problems for the time being to concentrate on the investigation again. "Marvellous news. We need to organise a surveillance team ASAP."

"Graham and Patrick have volunteered to be the first shout."

"What about their tasks?"

"The rest of the team have said they'll take up the slack, add them to their to-do lists."

"If everyone is okay with that suggestion then give them my blessing. Tell them to keep in touch if he's there or if he goes on the move at all."

"Of course I will."

Charlie left her to celebrate the news on her own with a bottle of water from her desk drawer. She spotted her roll from the day before and binned it.

She downed the contents of the bottle and then joined the others. Graham and Patrick had already left.

"Can we go over where we stand?"

The phone rang, and Charlie answered it. "Thanks, not what we wanted to hear. I'll pass on the news." She hung up and grimaced. "The blue Honda was spotted on a waste site this morning, burntout. The desk sergeant saw it on the wires and thought we'd better know ASAP."

"Great. Hey, let's not lose heart, at least we've got an address for Boyd, we don't need the vehicle."

"What if...?" Charlie began and stopped.

"Go on, Charlie."

"What if he dumped that car, torched it and stole another one close by?"

Katy pointed at her. "See, now that's what I call thinking outside the box. Can you do some digging in the system for me?"

"With pleasure. It's the only way I can think of him getting out of there."

"Either that or he got a cab, if it's near a main thoroughfare," Karen chipped in.

"Damn, I never thought of that," Charlie admitted.

"Another great suggestion. We can work both angles. Karen, can you ring round the many taxi firms in the area and see if any of the drivers picked James Boyd up. We'll need to trace his steps ready to fling at him during an interview and a possible court case. What am I saying? You're aware of that shit!"

Charlie smiled. "Leave us to it."

"I've chased up Forensics, they're going to do their best but they're up against it because of all the different crime scenes involved. Nothing in this life is easy, apparently. I know what I can do, call the hospital, see how Camilla is," Katy said as if justifying her need to be active. She raced back into the office and dropped into her chair. She glanced up to see Charlie standing in the doorway.

"Are you sure you're okay?"

"Don't I seem it? Oh no, you think my flighty behaviour is to do with the bump on my head. It's not, I promise."

"Okay, I was concerned for a moment there."

"I might as well tell you. Come in and shut the door. I called AJ. He told me Georgie was feeling under the weather, and my motherly guilt gene took on a life of its own."

Charlie placed her hands on the back of the spare chair and asked, "Define 'under the weather'?"

"A slight cold. She was tucked up in bed. I made AJ go and check on her while I was on the phone."

"Gosh, then I can see why you seem a bit anxious. She's in good hands with him."

"I know. I have no qualms in that department. We were told by her consultant to keep a close eye on her so, naturally, when she comes down with something, no matter how minor it might seem to others, to her, and her damaged heart, we could be talking about a life-or-death situation."

"Damn. I knew there was an underlying problem but I never knew how severe it was. No wonder you're fretting. Should you be here?"

Katy waved the question away. "Yeah, if I dropped everything and went home now, I don't think AJ would ever forgive me. I'd be stepping on his toes as her primary carer."

"A tough situation, I admit that. You two, your combined efforts are amazing. Georgie is a very lucky little girl."

"Thanks, Charlie, AJ has to take the main share of the credit, though. I refuse to hog the limelight when he does most of the hard work caring for her."

"It's a joint effort, stop putting yourself down."

"I'm not. All I'm being is truthful. Now get out of here, let's remain focused on the job in hand."

Charlie mock-saluted her and left the office.

Katy rang the hospital. Camilla had been placed on the women's ward in a private room. The nurse informed her they were keeping a constant eye on her. Camilla was tearful and obviously very upset by the loss of her fiancé but appeared to be bearing up well under the considerable strain she was under. Katy gave the nurse her number to call if things should change while Camilla was still in their care. The nurse promised she would, then hung up.

With vigour, Katy had breezed through the chore of dealing with the paperwork that had been lying in her in-tray. That left her free to lend her team a hand.

Karen discovered that James Boyd had since left Zedex, gone freelance and registered a firm with Companies House. That added up, and would have allowed him the time off to have committed the murders. Katy's spirits were lifted by the news which would add ammunition to their armoury when they pulled him in. Tracking his movements and being able to place him at the scene could be the key to putting him behind bars.

The boys reported in a few times during the day. Nothing, Boyd wasn't around. They'd even conducted a small house-to-house enquiry of the road to see if anyone had seen Boyd recently. The next-door neighbour told Graham and Patrick he hadn't seen James at the house in over a week. It wasn't the news Katy wanted to hear.

On the way home that evening, she called in at the hospital to have a brief chat with Camilla.

The young woman had red raw eyes. There was a bag of used tissues beside her bed. She glanced up and stared at Katy with glassy eyes. "Hello, aren't you the policewoman who…?"

"That's right. I was with you earlier."

Both of them skirted around the 'saved' word.

"I should thank you for what you did. The truth is, I can't figure out yet if what you did for me was a good or bad thing."

"I understand your confusion. It's been a tough day for you."

"It has. And here I am now, lying here, thinking…just reflecting on what we had."

"The struggle is going to be real for you during the coming weeks and months, but I believe you're strong enough to cope with what life is about to throw at you."

"How can you say that? I have so many doubts…you should've let me go…I wanted to be with him. Now what's going to happen to me? I'm going to die a lonely old woman. I can't be trusted to fall in love again…not while James is on the loose. You really think he's the one who did this?"

"Don't you? From what we've learned so far, it wouldn't make sense not to consider him as our main suspect. That's why I'm here, not to pressure you into speaking to me, but to see if you can help us track him down."

"How do you expect me to do that? I haven't seen him in ages, that was by choice." She nervously twisted a tissue through her fingers, and her gaze was drawn to her hands.

"I appreciate how hard this is for you. Don't you want us to catch him, Camilla?"

Her head shot up, and her eyes narrowed. "What sort of question is that? Of course I want him caught. I want you to lock him up and bury the damn key so he never sees the light of day again."

"My problem is that we've had a team sat outside his house all day, and he hasn't been near the place. He'd stolen a car to use to get him to the various crime scenes, but we discovered that burnt out earlier on a waste site. You see, although we're doing our very best to find him, we're struggling to locate him. In other words, he's proving elusive and we can't understand why."

Camilla shrugged. "What do you expect me to do about that? I'm sitting here in hospital after trying to commit suicide, and here you are, hounding me about the one man I detest the most in this world—no, make that *this universe*. I can't take this. You're pushing me closer to the edge again. I want you to leave." Her voice rose.

The next second, a nurse rushed into the room. "Everything all right in here?"

Katy's cheeks warmed under her intense gaze. "Yes, just a misunderstanding."

The nurse shifted, leaving a gap between herself and the hallway. "I think you should leave, Inspector, now. Mrs Boyd is in a fragile state. I knew it was wrong allowing you to see her so soon."

Katy's head dropped as the shame descended. "I'm sorry. Please forgive me, Camilla. The last thing I wanted to do was make your rehabilitation worse. All I'm trying to do is capture the man who has affected so many lives in the past thirty-six hours."

Camilla sniffed and wiped her runny nose. "No, I'm sorry. I appreciate you have a job to do." She let out a long breath. "I'm just tired. Tired of thinking what my future held, and now all I can consider is how lonely the world is going to be without him. Rufus, I mean."

The nurse approached the bed and puffed up the pillows behind her. "There, there, you don't have to talk. Just relax, there's no need for you to get yourself in a tizzy again."

"Is that a technical term?" Katy asked, smiling in an attempt to cut through the chilled atmosphere which had descended.

It worked. Camilla grinned. "I'm sorry for getting in a 'tizzy'. You have to understand that today...I lost everything. Rufus was my world..."

"Honestly, I get that. Please, won't you consider helping me by trying to find James?"

Camilla stared at the corner of the room for what appeared to be an eternity until she finally relented. "Okay, I'll help, for Rufus' sake."

Katy pulled up a chair.

The nurse patted Camilla's hand and said, "I'll leave you to it. Give me a shout if you need me."

"Thank you," Camilla replied.

Katy glanced up and nodded at the nurse. The door closed, leaving Katy alone with Camilla. "Please, hear me out. I'm going to try and make this as painless as possible. My intention isn't to cause you any more unnecessary anxiety. You're doing exceptionally well. If at any time you want to stop, that's fine by me."

"No, I think I'd like to get it over with in one go. I'm getting tired, my lids are drooping. What do you need to know?"

"When you were with James, was there a place he dearly liked to visit?"

"In the area?"

"Yes." She watched on as the woman's eyes narrowed and her head tilted as she thought. "Wait, maybe. I think his parents…no, I know his parents used to own a holiday cottage somewhere down on the coast. He was left it in his father's will. It was only a one-bedroom place. Now where was it?"

Katy kept quiet, giving Camilla the time and space to ponder.

Camilla eventually shook her head. "I can't for the life of me think where it was. There's definitely one around, though, if that's any help."

"We can do some digging. Did you ever go there?" Katy tried her best to jog the woman's memory.

"No. We were planning to, but things always went against us. Either bad weather or something cropped up at work to prevent us from going. In the end, we never got around to using it. Shame really, going away for the weekend might have helped save our marriage in the long run."

"You really believe that?"

She stared at the tissue in her hand. "I don't know. We led a boring life. His controlling behaviour destroyed my self-esteem. The one night I arranged to go out with the girls and I was fortunate to meet Rufus.

He sincerely turned my world upside down. I fell in love with him the first time I laid eyes on him. I know it was wrong of me as I was married at the time. But let's face it, if I'd been happy my eyes wouldn't have wandered."

"When you told James the marriage was over, what was his reaction?"

"I feel like you're testing me, asking me the same questions again. Like I said before, he accepted it. His demeanour didn't change. He didn't plead with me not to leave him. He didn't say that his world would collapse if I walked out on him, nothing! Therefore, I moved in with Rufus and we lived our lives to the fullest. He treated me like a princess. I know a lot of women say that about their fellas, but he truly did. He couldn't do enough for me. All our plans have now disintegrated. I'm lost without him. I can't see it getting easier anytime soon."

"Time is..."

"A great healer, yes, I've heard it all since coming in here. I'm afraid to shut my eyes. To dream, because I know he'll be there, holding my hand, waiting for me to join him on our next adventure. My dreams were always filled with him and the joy we shared. I know that sounds sloppy, it would to my ears if any of my friends spoke that way about their fella, but it doesn't alter the fact that Rufus was a very special guy. I will miss him...more than life itself. I know I was foolish." She ran a finger over the bandage decorating her left wrist.

"You won't try it again, will you?" Katy asked quietly.

She shook her head. "I don't think so. My head wasn't in the right place at the time. I shudder at the thought of taking that razor in my right hand and...I've never considered doing anything as bad as that before..."

"Grief is a powerful emotion to deal with. It's very much taken for granted by most people. It can tear a person apart in an unexpected way. Words are cheap. No one can define a person's future for them after suffering a great loss such as losing the love of their life. I wouldn't begin to try. All I can advise is for you to hang in there. You seem a bit brighter than before."

"I think I've had time to reflect, which has helped immensely—that is until the seeds of guilt hit me. What if I hadn't met him on that night out? Would Rufus still be alive today? Of course he would. It's my fault he's dead. If he hadn't taken me under his wing, sheltered me and cured my shattered nerves, he'd still be alive. That type of guilt will take its toll on a person."

"Hmm...no one will be able to right that wrong, but I don't think you should feel guilty about it. Life just got in the way, nothing more than that."

"I know. Maybe in time I'll be able set those feelings aside and learn to deal with life again, not now, but definitely in the future."

"That's the spirit. I'm sure, once we've captured James, things will look so much brighter. It won't make things right, of course, but it'll lessen the blow, if I can put it that way."

Camilla nodded. "I hope so. I'm tired now. Do you need anything else from me?"

"I don't think so. You get some rest. I'll leave you my card. If you can recall any other places James loved to visit in the past, maybe you can give me a ring."

"I'll do that. Do you think he'll come after me?" she asked with a sleepy yawn.

"I don't think so. As soon as you're well enough to leave the hospital, I'll personally take you to the safe house."

"You'd do that for me?"

Katy rose from her chair and rubbed Camilla's arm. "I would. Do you need me to send the nurse in to help you get more comfortable?"

"No. I'll be fine. Thank you for caring about me. It means a lot."

"No problem. Wishing you a speedy recovery. I'll keep in touch with the nursing staff. As soon as the doctor gives you the all clear to leave, I'll drop by and pick you up, how's that?"

"Thank you." She was gone, drifted off to sleep like an innocent baby.

Katy left the room and walked up to the nurses' station. "She's asleep. I've left my card should she need me. You're aware of what's happened today, I take it?"

The two nurses on duty both nodded.

"I'm going to place a uniformed officer outside her door, if that's okay with you?"

"I was about to suggest the same," the nurse who'd visited Camilla's room earlier said.

"Here's my card. Should you need me, just shout."

"We'll do that."

Katy bade them farewell and made her way through the endless winding corridors back to her vehicle. En route, she rang the station and requested the desk sergeant to send one of his team to stand guard outside Camilla's room, something, had her mind been fully on the job, she should have arranged a couple of hours earlier. *Never mind, it's done now, finally! Time to call it a day.*

She arrived home, with the flow of traffic in her favour for a change, to find AJ in the kitchen. He was at the table, going over some paperwork. She kissed the top of his head, startling him.

"Damn, I was so engrossed I didn't hear you come in."

He pulled her onto his lap and kissed her, long and hard. Enough for all her troubles and woes to vanish momentarily.

"That's a nice welcome, thank you. How's the little one? I need to go and see her." She struggled to get off his lap.

But he clung to her. "Five minutes won't hurt. She's fine. I checked on her a few minutes ago."

She wrapped her arms around his neck. "You truly are the best dad ever. What are you up to?"

"I thought I'd make a start on keeping my accounts in order right from the word go. It makes sense, doesn't it?"

"Too right it does, especially as your main role is looking after Georgie. Anything you can do to keep things organised has to be a bonus."

"Yep, that's what I thought, too. Mmm…however, it's kind of got in the way of me cooking dinner."

"No problem. We'll rustle up something together. What's in the fridge?" She leapt off his lap and wandered across the room and pulled open the door. Staring back at her were all the makings of a frittata. "I know. If you give me a hand preparing the ingredients, we could be eating within half an hour."

He crept up behind her and nuzzled into her neck. "Teamwork, always a bonus in my book."

Within ten minutes they had all the ingredients chopped, and Katy placed the onions in the frying pan to sweat a little before throwing in the diced peppers and chopped-up bacon pieces. She sprinkled in a few herbs and then whisked up five eggs, added a dash of Worcester sauce and a splash of milk and poured it over the rest. AJ lit the grill, and after a couple of minutes Katy shoved the pan under it and went to the cutlery drawer.

She handed AJ the knives and forks, and he laid the table and opened a bottle of red wine. "Naughty during the week, but it won't hurt us once in a while." She smiled and took a sip of the fruity wine. "Lovely. Just what I needed after today."

"Want to share?"

"Not really. I'd rather forget all about it and concentrate on us. Can you watch the frittata doesn't burn? I need to get changed and I'll pop in and see Georgie at the same time."

"Go. I'll turn it down if it gets too hot."

Katy tiptoed up the stairs, she wasn't sure why. Once Georgie was asleep, an erupting volcano couldn't wake her. She crept across the room. The nightlight was on beside her bed. Her daughter was sleeping peacefully. She kissed her on the cheek and brushed the hair back from her face. Georgie's skin was clammy, hot and sticky. She placed a hand on her forehead, and her heart sank and her blood ran cold. Her legs shaking, she ran to the top of the stairs and called AJ.

He bounded into the room.

By this time, Katy was kneeling beside her daughter. "I don't like what I'm seeing, love. Did you take her temperature before she went to bed?"

"No. I didn't think to. Is she hot?" He felt her head and stared at Katy. "I swear she wasn't that bad earlier. Oh God! What have I done?"

"Hush now. You haven't done anything wrong. It could be nothing.

Get a small towel from the airing cupboard and run it under the cold tap. We'll try and bring her temperature down that way, wake her up and give her Calpol."

AJ darted out of the room. Katy threw the bedclothes back and checked her daughter over from head to foot. She found it weird that Georgie's hands and feet were as cold as ice and yet the rest of her was burning up. Katy scrambled for her phone and Googled the symptoms. She gasped when the results came back. AJ entered the room and placed the towel over Georgie's forehead. Katy read on. *Shit! No way, this can't be...* She undid Georgie's PJ top and discovered a rash on her daughter's tummy. Katy grabbed the glass of water on the side table and ran out of the room. She emptied the contents in the bathroom sink and sprinted back to join AJ.

"What's going on? Katy, you're scaring me."

"Wait. If the rash doesn't alter when pressed, then we're in trouble."

"What? Why? Oh fuck! It's not meningitis, is it?"

"It could be." Katy pressed the glass against her daughter's skin, and the rash remained the same.

"Shit." She rang one-one-one in a panic.

"Hello, you're through to the NHS helpline, how can I help?"

"I think my five-year-old daughter has meningitis."

"Okay, I need you to remain calm while I go through a list of questions."

"Please hurry."

"I'll be as quick as I can." The woman started reeling off the questions one after the other, and Katy's response to them all was affirmative.

"I need you to listen very carefully."

"I am. Please, hurry."

"I'm going to ask you to take your daughter to hospital right away, no delay, you need to go the minute I end this call."

"Oh God, I'm right, aren't I?"

"It definitely sounds like it to me. Remain calm, you've got this."

Suddenly the fire alarm sounded downstairs. AJ shot out of the room.

"What's that?" the woman asked.

"My dinner burning. Don't worry about it, my child is more important."

"Okay. Is someone dealing with your dinner?"

"My husband. Should I go to St Thomas'?"

"Yes, do that. I'll let them know you're on your way. Promise me you'll drive safely."

"I will. I promise. I've just come from the hospital. I was visiting a patient there. Sorry, I'm waffling. My poor baby, will she survive?"

"You have to believe. If you've caught it early enough there's no reason why she can't kick this into touch."

"Thank you for all your help. I'm going to get her in the car now."

"You do that. Take care. I'll ensure the hospital are aware of your imminent arrival."

AJ came back into the room. "Dinner is no longer." He seemed shell-shocked and tears sparkled in his eyes.

"Thank you," Katy replied to the woman on control. She ended the call and stood. "We need to get her to St Thomas', love."

"Damn. Why didn't I think to check her for a rash?"

"Enough. We're not going to start blaming ourselves, you hear me?"

AJ swept Georgie into his arms. Katy followed him down the stairs and snatched her car keys off the console table. She opened the front door for AJ to carry Georgie out to the car and then locked it behind her.

AJ placed their daughter in the back seat. "You get in there with her. It'll be easier to strap you both in."

"Are you going to be okay to drive?"

"Yep, I'm focused on getting us there, nothing else. We've got this, love. Don't fret."

AJ sat in the back and held Georgie against him then pulled the seat belt around both of them. It was a snug fit, even Katy knew it was the wrong way to be travelling. "Are you comfy? Maybe she should be in her car seat?"

"She's secure with me. It's only twenty minutes away. The quicker we get on the road..."

"I can take a hint. Do me a favour and place your knees into the back of the passenger seat just in case."

"Go. We're wasting time. Nothing is going to happen if you concentrate on your driving."

Katy inhaled a large breath and set off.

True to the word of the woman on control, when they arrived at Accident and Emergency there was a team of three nurses and a doctor waiting for them beside a trolley.

"Hi, I rang earlier about my daughter," Katy shouted. She opened the back door and helped AJ undo his seat belt.

"We'll take it from here," the young male doctor replied.

AJ and Katy followed the staff up the corridor and into triage. They were prevented from entering the room and asked to wait in the family room instead.

The wait seemed to go on forever. Katy prayed to God to save Georgie, to even consider swapping places with her sick child. She clung to AJ for moral support. It turned out he needed it as much as she did.

"Should we ring our parents?" Katy said reluctantly.

"Let's leave it for now. Get the diagnosis and go from there. We might be wrong about this."

"I don't think so, but yes, you're right. Until we have the diagnosis it would be best not to ring them. AJ, I'm scared. She's all we've got."

He cradled her in his arms and soothed a hand over her hair. "Think positive. She's a fighter, look at what she's already been through..."

She sniffed. "That's what's worrying me. Does she have it in her to fight something so dangerous after what her heart has already suffered over the years? I'm not so sure." She let out a shuddering breath, and an imaginary hand clutched her heart. She rubbed at the pain between her breasts.

"Are you all right? What is it?"

"Nothing. My heart is in pieces and it's painful, that's all."

AJ hugged her tighter. "Stick with me, babe, we'll get through this together. All three of us. We're a team, nothing is going to tear us apart. I promise you."

The doctor entered the room. One look at his expression, and Katy's legs gave way beneath her. AJ guided her to a nearby chair.

"I'm sorry to tell you that your daughter does indeed have meningitis. I'm not one to beat around the bush, so forgive me if you think my bedside manner is non-existent."

"Nonsense. We'd rather have the facts straight, Doctor," AJ replied.

"Right you are then. I believe your daughter has bacterial meningitis as opposed to viral. We'll be moving her to the Intensive Care Unit soon. You're welcome to stay with her, but I want you to be aware that it could take a while for her to show any signs of improvement. Has she complained about having a headache or any stiffness to her limbs in the past few days? Possibly squinting at the lights or glare from the TV screen?"

Katy and AJ glanced at each other and shrugged.

"I don't think so. She developed the sniffles today, and I put her to bed early. I checked on Georgie just before my wife came home from work, and she seemed settled enough. My wife looked in on her and discovered she had a fever and a rash. It was that quick," AJ replied.

Katy was grateful AJ was here, her brain had turned to mush. Her baby was seriously ill, and here she was, numb and unsure what to ask for the best. She had the urge to run to be with Georgie, not to hang around listening to the doctor's words which were coming out jumbled now.

"That's often the case. At least you got her here swiftly. That's imperative in cases such as this. Please, try not to worry."

"What about her heart?" Katy muttered.

"I'm aware she has ongoing issues. We'll monitor her every step of the way. Now, if you'll excuse me, I need to get your daughter settled in ICU ASAP."

"Of course. Thank you for giving us an update so quickly, Doctor." AJ shook his hand.

The doctor left the room. AJ dropped into the chair next to Katy. They stared at each other, and then AJ touched his forehead against hers, and they cried together.

After a few minutes of feeling sorry for herself, Katy reached into her handbag and pulled out a tissue for each of them.

"It's imperative we remain strong, Katy."

Katy wiped her eyes and then her nose. "I know. It's going to be so difficult. What if…?"

AJ wagged a finger. "Those words are not to be used, not this time. Shit, we'd better call our parents, they'll be livid if they find out we're here and we didn't call them."

"I can't think about that for now. I need to be with her, AJ."

"We'll make our way up there in a few minutes. Let me make the calls first."

"I'm not sure what I'd do if you weren't here to support me."

He touched her cheek. She sighed as more tears fell.

"Stay strong, Katy. We've got this, sweetheart. She's in the best place, thanks to you."

Katy frowned. "I'm not having that. We both did well getting her here."

"Yeah, but if…"

She placed a finger on his lips to silence him. "Teamwork, nothing more and nothing less than that, AJ. Haven't you got some calls to make? No, correction, you call your parents and I'll ring mine." A sudden inner strength came to the fore.

AJ smiled. "That's my girl, welcome back."

Katy went to the other side of the room and called her parents. Her mother shrieked the second she told her. "Mum, please, try to calm down. The doctor praised us for getting her here so quickly. She's in the best place possible to make a recovery."

"And will she? Recover? What sort of strain is this going to put on her heart?"

"We won't know that for a few days. She's safe for now, Mum. I just wanted to let you know."

"Thank you for ringing me. Do you want me to come down there?"

"No, there's no point. She'll be in hospital for at least a couple of days, I should imagine, although that has yet to be confirmed."

"All right. Ring me with regular updates, if you get the time."

"I will, I promise. Love you, Mum."

"We love you, too, dear. Give our little princess a gentle hug when you can. Stay strong, Katy. I'll say an extra prayer for you all this evening."

"It'll be appreciated. Thanks, Mum."

Katy ended the call and walked over to AJ who was rolling his eyes as he spoke to his parents. He put the phone on speaker. "Mother, you need to calm down. We're responsible adults. Katy and I got Georgie here quickly, that's going to make all the difference to how she responds to the treatment."

"Can you guarantee that? Can the doctors? What about going private? We've got a policy, I'm sure it will cover you and your family. I can dig it out and have a look."

"Mum, we're in safe hands here. Thanks for the offer, but we've got this. I'm just calling you to give you an update on what's happening."

"I know you are. The offer is still on the table, should you need it."

"Thanks. I've got to go, the doctor is here to speak to us," he lied, just to get rid of her.

"Oh, very well. Keep me informed. I could be there within the hour, if you should want me, us."

"Let's see how things progress for now. There are only usually two visitors to a bed anyway."

"I'm glad you're together. Stay positive, and let me know daily if you can."

"I will. Goodbye, Mother."

AJ wrapped an arm around Katy's shoulders and pulled her in for a hug. "That's the hard part done, now we can concentrate on our daughter."

"I need to ring Roberts. Make him aware of the situation and that I won't be able to work for a few days."

"Let's hold fire on that for now."

They hugged again and drifted into the corridor, stopping a porter to ask the way to ICU. He dished out instructions, and they set off.

At the nurses' station in ICU, one of the nurses gave them both gowns and masks to wear. Georgie was there already, behind a screen as they were setting up the equipment for her. The screen was removed around fifteen minutes later. Katy gasped. Her daughter was hooked up to several monitors, an IV drip, and she was wearing an oxygen mask.

The nurse who had given them the gowns placed an arm around her waist. "It looks worse than it is, I promise. Come on."

Katy and AJ held hands and approached Georgie's bed.

Katy's eyes misted. She wiped the moisture away to clear her vision. "My poor baby."

"Hush now, think positively, love," AJ whispered and kissed the top of her head.

The nurse placed two chairs on the other side of the bed and motioned for them to sit down. "What about a drink? Can I get you a tea or coffee?"

Katy shook her head. "No, you have enough to do as it is, without running around after us."

"Nonsense. It's a one-time-only offer, we do it for all new arrivals. You're on your own after that." The nurse smiled and winked.

"Okay, you've twisted my arm. Two coffees, milk with one sugar. Thank you so much."

"No problem. I'll be right back."

Katy and AJ took their seats.

Katy stared at her daughter, willing her to get better, and quickly. "She seems so fragile."

"She does. She'll pull through this. We have to believe that."

"I'm doing my best to think positively, but it's not easy when you consider what she's been through in the past."

"Even more so, she came through that last time. Surprising both of us. She's a resilient little bugger."

Katy smiled. "She is."

The nurse reappeared. "Here you go. I'm Maddie, by the way."

"Thanks, Maddie. AJ and Katy."

"Pleased to meet you. If you have any questions at all, don't hesitate to ask any one of us. There's always someone around."

"You're too kind. Is it all right if we hang around?"

"For a few hours. You should go home and get some rest when you can. She's monitored all the time, so there's really no need for you to be concerned at this stage."

"Do many children die from this?"

The nurse smiled. "Not really. Not nowadays. The statistics are in Georgina's favour."

"It's Georgie," Katy whispered. "My little Georgie, and she's a fighter."

"I have no doubt about that. I'll be over there if you need me."

"You're very kind, thank you."

The next couple of hours consisted of deep sighs and a lot of hand holding. Eventually, at around midnight, AJ suggested they should go home. Katy detested the thought of leaving her daughter there alone, but the nurse assured them it was their best option and to get some rest. In the end, Katy gave in. AJ drove home, and everything was carried out on autopilot, Katy's mind elsewhere, with her daughter.

"What are you going to do about work?" AJ asked once they were in bed.

"I'm going to play it by ear. See what tomorrow brings."

"I'll ring the hospital first thing, eh?"

"I was thinking the same. What a day."

Katy drifted off to sleep, exhausted.

8

*N*either she nor AJ slept well that night. He got up and made a drink while she called the hospital to see how Georgie had fared overnight. She spoke to a different nurse who had an equally pleasing manner about her. The nurse told her that Georgie had slept well during the night and seemed to be a little better that morning. Her temperature was coming down by the hour, which was a huge relief. The nurse added a note of caution that it wasn't uncommon for temperatures to spike now and again during the infection.

With that news on board, she rang DCI Roberts. He appeared to have just got up and sounded annoyed to receive a call from her so early.

"What is it, Katy? Couldn't this wait until nine?"

"No, sir. You know I wouldn't be ringing you at this hour if it wasn't important."

"Go on then."

"Would it be possible for me to have some time off?"

"What? You've only just come back to work after your damn honeymoon. Off on your jollies again so soon?"

"Hardly, sir. It's Georgie."

"What about her? Is she all right?" Concern was obvious in his voice.

"She's in hospital. She's got meningitis."

"Jesus Christ, why didn't you tell me that sooner rather than sitting there, letting me tear you off a strip?"

"I'm still trying to get my head around it myself, sir. It's hard to say the word, as you can imagine."

"Of course. Oh, Katy, I'm so sorry. What's the prognosis?"

"Not sure as yet. They're monitoring her. We were initially worried about the effect it would have on her heart."

"Of course, she's not a well child anyway, this on top will only add to your stress. Yes, take all the time off you need."

"Thank you. I'll see how things go for now."

"Keep me informed. Sending my best wishes to the little one and to you and AJ."

"What about the case?"

"I'll step in. Don't worry. Charlie and I will deal with it."

"Christ, poor Charlie… Umm…that came out wrong, what I meant was that she has her sergeant's exam in a few days."

"She'll be fine. That's the least of your concerns. Just concentrate on getting Georgie better and out of hospital. All right if I inform the team? Or would you rather keep it quiet?"

"No, you can tell them. Good luck with the investigation, sir. At least we know who the killer is, it's just a matter of tracking him down."

"You've done all the hard work, leave it to us to find him."

"Thanks for being so understanding, Sean. I truly appreciate it."

"Ring me later, if you get the chance."

"I will."

Katy ended the call and released the breath she'd been holding in. "That's a relief. He's going to take over the case for a few days."

AJ placed the tray on the bed and slipped in beside her. "Thank God for that. One less thing for you to worry about."

"This means we can visit Georgie together, the onus isn't solely on your shoulders."

"I know how you feel about work and how involved you get with your investigations. If you need to be there, you have my blessing, you know that."

She leaned over and kissed him. "I know. Let's see what today brings first."

~

*C*harlie arrived at work at around ten-to-nine and entered the incident room to find DCI Roberts pacing the floor in front of the whiteboard. Patrick and Stephen were already at their desks.

"Come in, Charlie. Any sign of the rest of the team?"

"Karen's nipped to the loo. She shouldn't be long. Is everything okay, sir?"

"Not really. I'll share the news once everyone is here."

Five minutes later and he did just that. "The more observant amongst you will have noticed that Inspector Foster isn't with us today. She rang me first thing with some devastating news." He raised a hand for the others to let him finish as several mouths opened to ask the obvious question. "It's her daughter, Georgie. She's been admitted to hospital with meningitis. Katy has asked for a few days off, therefore, I'll be stepping in to take over the case. Any objections?"

"Why would we, sir?" Charlie challenged.

"Good. You'll have the pleasure of me being your partner for the foreseeable future, Charlie, and yes, I'm aware you have an exam to sit at the end of the week. We'll deal with that nearer the time. So, who would like to bring me up to date on where we're at with the investigation?"

Between them, the team filled him in.

"So the surveillance proved to be a waste of time. This cottage that Katy got out of the ex-wife, has anyone had a chance to follow up on that yet?"

"No, Katy only sent me a text last night once she'd left the hospital. That needs to be our priority, however, if I might add, sir, I don't think we should throw much weight behind it."

His brow furrowed. "Why?"

"Because all the murders have taken place in this area, not on the coast where the cottage is situated."

"Makes sense. Good thinking, Charlie, that's probably saved us a few hours of travelling down there and it proving to be a waste of time."

"I have my uses, sir." Charlie grinned.

"You do. Let's try and source the address and leave it to one side for now. If he senses us getting close, he might resort to using that place in the future, agreed?"

"Agreed," Charlie replied. Want us to get on with the tasks we were set yesterday by Inspector Foster?"

"Yes, let's up the pace. Do we know if everything was quiet overnight, or if any other murders have taken place? I hope I'm not tempting fate by mentioning that."

"I'll do the necessary checks with the desk sergeant. Karen, can you check the wires for me?" Charlie asked.

Karen nodded, and her fingers flitted across the keyboard. "Nope, nothing as yet."

Charlie breathed out a relieved sigh. She picked up a nearby phone and contacted the reception desk. The sergeant told her all had been as silent as a graveyard there as well. She reported back to Roberts.

"That's good news. What other leads do we have that we can be working on today?"

Charlie raised her hand. "I was in the process of searching the database for any possible stolen cars in the area where Boyd's previously acquired vehicle was found."

"Makes sense. Get back to that, Charlie. Let's hit the ground running and have this bastard behind bars quickly."

He marched into Katy's office and closed the door.

Charlie took it upon herself to buy him a coffee and delivered it a few seconds later. She knocked on the door. He yelled for her to enter.

Roberts glanced up from the brown envelopes littered across the desk. "Damn post, gets more and more each day. Is that for me?"

"It is, sir. Thought it would help you tackle this lot."

"Are you sucking up, Simpkins?"

Charlie's cheeks warmed. "No, sir. The thought never even crossed my mind. If you don't want it, I'll have it."

"I was jesting. Thank you for being so thoughtful. Time to see what the inspector is always complaining about." He took a sip and grimaced. "Crikey, no wonder she's always on the cadge for a decent Colombian coffee when she visits my office."

"It's decent enough, sir. You get used to it after a while."

"Depends whether your taste buds survive in the meantime, I should think. Thank you anyway. Let me know if anything comes to light out there. I'll be a while going through this lot, I should imagine."

"Yes, sir. Do you mind if I ask how Katy sounded when you spoke to her?"

"She seemed to be bearing up. That doesn't mean to say that you should be pestering her. Leave her alone for a day or so. Send her a text to let her know you're thinking about her, if you have to. It might be a good idea if you did that, let her know that you care."

"Thanks for the advice, sir. I'll crack on and leave you to your onerous chore."

"Great. I can't wait to get stuck in to someone else's pile of crap."

Charlie smiled and backed out of the office. She made her way back to her desk and fired off a text to Katy to let her know that she and the team were thinking about her.

Katy responded within a few minutes.

We're fine. Be in touch soon. Thank you, and good luck with Roberts!

Charlie smiled, aware she may need to keep her spirits up with the main man sitting only a few feet away from her. *Christ! Mum would be laughing her socks off now if she knew this was happening.* She pondered whether she should call her mother regarding

Georgie or not. It could wait until that evening when she finished her shift, providing she made it home that night.

Another half an hour flew by before she had a list of vehicles Boyd might have picked up for the next leg of his mission. There was no telling what that was likely to be, but at least they'd have a heads-up on him, for now.

Roberts came out of the office and deposited his cup in the waste bin close to the vending machine. "Best place for it, I think. I'll try and find another supplier. Bear with me on that one, won't you, guys?"

"Sounds good to us, sir," Patrick shouted.

"Right, what have we got?"

Charlie was the first to speak. "I've made a list of all the vehicles stolen within a couple of miles of the location where he dumped the last car."

"Good, good. Any luck tracing those vehicles through either the CCTV or ANPRs in the area?"

"Stephen and Patrick are looking into that now, sir."

The phone on Karen's desk rang. She answered it. Her face dropped as she glanced at Charlie. She hung up and shook her head. "Yet another shooting."

"Where?" Roberts asked.

"In the underground car park at Zedex."

"What? Why hasn't that place been sealed off by now?" Roberts demanded.

"Would that have been feasible, sir?" Karen asked.

"Charlie, you and I should get over there. I take it the pathologist is at the scene?"

"Yes, and SOCO, sir," Karen replied.

"Carry on with the tasks in hand. We'll bring you up to date on things when we return. Charlie, are you ready?"

"I was born ready," Charlie replied and winced when the words tumbled out of her mouth.

"I'm not surprised, considering who spawned you."

Charlie stifled the laugh teetering on her tongue.

. . .

*R*oberts drove, and they arrived at the scene within twenty-five minutes. "I might be a bit rusty out in the field, feel free to butt in at any time."

"Don't worry, sir, I've got your back," Charlie replied cheekily.

Patti eyed them with curiosity. "Hello, what's going on here? And you are?"

"DCI Roberts, Patti, he's my partner for the day."

"Something wrong with Katy?" Patti asked.

"Can we keep to the investigation in hand?" Roberts interjected.

"Of course. Yet another victim who worked for Zedex. Apparently, she was on the phone to her fiancée at the time. You've got good camera angles, hopefully you'll manage to pick something up from them."

"Her name is Andrea Gregory," Charlie filled in, staring at the body.

"Thanks. I'll note it down. If you want a closer look, I'm going to have to ask you to suit up to protect the crime scene."

"That won't be necessary," Roberts said. "We'll leave you to it and track down the camera footage. Nice to meet you, by the way, Patti, I've often heard you mentioned."

"I'm at a disadvantage; that's a good thing, right? Proves the girls don't run you down, not within earshot of me."

Charlie sniggered.

"Good to hear I'm not the ogre they perceive me to be. This way to the office, is it?" Roberts pointed off to the left.

"I believe so."

"Don't let us hold you up then, Patti. I'll expect your PM report within the next day or two." He turned and walked away.

Patti raised an eyebrow and jerked her thumb in his direction. "I'll do my best," she shouted after him.

"You'll do more than that," he retorted.

Charlie watched the interaction and found it comical.

"DC Simpkins, are you coming?" Roberts bellowed, his voice echoing around the car park.

"Sorry, gotta fly."

"Good luck, Charlie."

"Thanks."

Charlie trotted to catch up with Roberts' long strides.

"Let's get one thing straight, I don't take to people standing around gossiping when there's information to gather and get collated," he said.

"I don't think we were gossiping as such, sir. Patti is a close friend. She's professional in the same way as we are, when we're involved in a case."

"Good, I'm relieved to hear that. Let's see what the camera tells us. They never lie, apparently."

They reached a tiny office. A man with chunky grey eyebrows answered the door. "You the police? Those people told me to expect you. I'm Warren Bagshaw."

Charlie showed her badge and introduced them. "Can you let us see the footage and perhaps run us off a copy of the disc?"

"Aye, I thinks I can do that for ye. Come in, although it'll be a bit of a squeeze with all three of us in here."

"I'm sure we'll manage," Roberts told him, sporting an uncomfortable grin. "Can you tell us when the body was discovered?"

"Right you are then. I've done my bit and set it up for you. I likes to be organised, you see. Didn't get to where I am today without being prepared. Yep, I came on duty at around eight. It wasn't until I did my rounds that I found her lying there. I suppose by the time I'd made a cup of coffee, drunk that, it must have been about eight-thirty."

"I see. If you'd like to start playing the disc. Thanks," Roberts requested.

Comparable to a sardine in the confined space, Warren started the disc. On the screen, Andrea arrived in the garage with a couple of colleagues.

"Do you recognise the other two?" Roberts whispered.

"Yes, Ben Thompson and Steve Abbott," Charlie responded without hesitation.

Warren nodded. "She's good and she's right," he confirmed. "This is where it gets interesting." He pointed at the monitor.

The two men waved farewell, and one after the other, their vehicles left the garage. Andrea was waylaid because she was on the phone. She laughed and smiled broadly all the time she spoke.

"Why didn't she just get in the damn car?" Charlie muttered. She shook her head, aware of what was about to happen next.

"Makes you wonder, doesn't it?" Roberts asked in response.

"She quite often does it," Warren added.

"I see, okay, so if it's a regular occurrence, then possibly the killer knew this and waited patiently for his chance to come."

"Here he is now," Warren announced.

A man came into shot wearing a clown's mask. He stood to the side of Andrea for a good few seconds. Being so engrossed in her conversation, she failed to notice him. He moved a few steps ahead of her, and she screamed, almost dropped the phone. The masked man applauded and tipped his head back, obviously laughing at her.

"Bastard, he got a real kick out of this before he finally did the deed," Charlie said.

"Aye, you could say that. Watch," Warren advised.

The man pointed at the ground. Andrea dropped her phone down by her side and got down on her knees in front of him. The woman, rightly so, looked shit-scared of what was about to happen to her. The masked man aimed a gun at her chest. It went off three times. Andrea fell to her side and lay there, dead. But that wasn't enough for the man. Whereas other killers might have done the business and run, fearing they might be caught, he remained there for a while. It was hard to tell what was going on, but Charlie presumed he was holding a conversation with the victim.

The murderer bent low and wagged the finger of his free hand while still aiming his gun at the dead Andrea. Then, he seemed to pause, pace the area for a few seconds before he directed the gun at the back of her head and shot her again, twice.

"Oh shit! That was a bit extreme, the woman was obviously already dead," Roberts murmured.

"I'd say so. Heartless piece of shit. We need to find him, and quickly," Charlie said.

"That's it. He takes off in a mo and doesn't even look back." Warren fast-forwarded the disc a little.

"Did he get away by car or on foot?" Roberts asked.

"Foot, I believe. I tried to pick him up on different cameras, but he disappeared as if he knew where the cameras were and how to avoid them," Warren said. He messed around with the buttons and then ejected the disc. "There you go." He placed the disc in a plastic case and handed it to Roberts.

"Much appreciated, thanks. A uniformed officer will drop by in a day or so to take a statement from you, if that's all right?"

"Aye, I'll be here. I'm here between eight in the morning and eight at night most days, except the weekends. This place is locked up then."

"One last question," Charlie said. "This all happened at around eight, after you left, I take it? How is the car park locked up at night?"

"I'd not long knocked off for the night. There are automatic gates, they come down at eight- thirty. Everyone knows they have to be out five minutes before that. It bugs me that the woman spent all night here alone. Maybe she was still alive, you know, after the shooting."

"I doubt it. Try not to let it eat away at you." Charlie rubbed at his arm.

They bid the man farewell and made their way back to Patti. She was examining the corpse.

"We've seen the disc. She was shot three times in the chest then, after a while, the fucker seemed to be having a conversation with her. Once he'd finished, he fired off another two shots in the back of her head."

"Sounds about right, I came to the conclusion that's how it must have gone down. Poor woman, maybe she pleaded for her life."

"I think she did, who knows?" Charlie said. "She was a nice lady. Katy and I interviewed her a few days ago, and now she's joined the victim list. This bastard is working his way through his previous colleagues, that's how it looks to me."

"Whoa, if you believe that, how many are left?" Patti asked.

"The two men we saw accompanying her to the car park, Ben and Steve, they parted and left for home. She was engaged in a conversation on her phone. She must have been distracted. I think if she'd seen the perpetrator she would have started running," Charlie filled the blanks in for Patti.

"Jesus. If only she'd got in her car and driven away, maybe she'd still be alive today."

Roberts agreed with Patti's assumption. "Too late to consider that now. We're wasting time. We need to get back to base and get things actioned."

Charlie cleared her throat.

"Something wrong, Charlie?" Roberts asked.

"We can't return to the station just yet, sir, we have an important task to perform."

He shook his head. "I'm not attending a post-mortem, if that's what you're suggesting."

"I wasn't. We need to go and pay the deceased's next of kin a visit. Let them know of her passing before the press get a hold of the news and start spouting about it."

He bashed his thigh with a clenched fist. "I told you I was rusty, yes, of course we should do that as a priority. Do we have an address for the victim?"

"I'll get in touch with Karen, see what she can find out for me." Charlie stepped away from Patti and Roberts and exhaled. She rang the station, and Karen supplied her with the address almost immediately. Charlie hung up and returned to where Patti and Roberts were discussing the ins and outs of why the perp would overkill his victim.

"Anger, there's no other explanation," Patti said.

"There are other ways of dealing with pent-up emotions other than killing people," Roberts was quick to suggest.

"Yep, not everyone realises that," Patti agreed. "I need to get on. Nice meeting you, DCI Roberts."

"You, too, Patti. Thanks for looking after my team so well. Keep up the good work."

Patti smirked. "I'll do my best. I hope you locate this bastard soon."

"We're going to do our very best, aren't we, DC Simpkins?"

"We are, sir."

Charlie and Roberts jumped back in his vehicle. He asked Charlie to punch the address into the satnav, and set off.

"I've just had a thought," she said.

Roberts turned to face her. "What about?"

"The phone call she was making. She was laughing, seemed really happy. What if she was on the phone to her next of kin at the time?"

Roberts groaned. "Damn, you're right, this could be a sticky situation."

"Sticky? We could be in the same boat as we were with Camilla."

"I'm not with you?"

"Camilla attempted to kill herself when it sank in that her fiancé was dead."

"Fuck. Hang on tight." Roberts pushed his foot down on the accelerator, and the car surged forward. He also flicked on the siren and weaved in and out of the traffic until they reached their destination.

Andrea had lived in a small terraced house in a quiet suburban street. Roberts found a parking space easily enough, something Charlie thought was probably a rarity come six p.m.

Charlie rang the bell.

A young woman in her early thirties with bloodshot eyes opened the door. "Yes?"

Charlie produced her warrant card. "DCI Roberts and DC Simpkins. Can we come in and have a brief word?"

"If it's about Andrea, you're hours too late. What the hell has taken you so long?"

"Sorry, we were only told about the incident this morning. What can you tell us about it?"

She stood back and allowed them to enter the hallway. "Come through to the lounge."

Roberts closed the front door, and Charlie followed the woman up the hallway into a room at the back. Lying on a big squishy bed was a golden retriever, wagging its tail. Charlie paused to pet the dog and then sat on the sofa next to Roberts as instructed by the woman.

"I don't think I caught your name," Charlie said.

"I didn't give it. It's Maria Miller. Andrea and I were engaged to be married. The registry office is all booked, the wedding venue, everything was in place and now…she's gone."

"We truly are sorry for your loss. Was she on the phone to you when she lost her life?" Charlie asked.

"When she was murdered, you mean. Yes. We were flirting. All that is gone now, I don't even have that as a lasting memory of her. All I have is her pleading for her damn life. Why? Why her? She's never done anyone any harm. Why would someone strip her of years of happiness within two minutes of meeting her?"

"We believe she knew the murderer."

"No! Who is it?"

"We think it's James Boyd, a former colleague of hers."

"Shit! I knew him, or should I say, of him. Why? He left the firm not long ago from what I can remember."

"You're right, he did."

"Why kill her, she never did him any harm?"

"That was going to be my next question, had they fallen out at all?"

"No, not really. He was up for promotion. A woman got in ahead of him, maybe that's what he objected to. Are you telling me that the two deaths which have already happened there, Grace and Colin being killed, were down to him?"

"That's what we believe, yes."

"Bloody hell. What does that say about our society? If you're given the sack…hang on, he wasn't even sacked, not from what I can recall. How sick is that?"

"We believe he left Zedex and set up his own rival firm in the last couple of months."

Maria frowned. "Rival firm? So he thought he'd wipe out the people he worked with at his prior firm to gain an advantage, is that right? Or am I missing something here?"

"I think you're going along the right lines. We need to track him down and get his take on things before the investigation makes any sense," Charlie said. She cast an eye sideways at Roberts who was nodding.

Damn, say something. Don't leave it all to me.

As if reading her mind, Roberts asked a question. "Were you together long?"

Charlie groaned inwardly. *What type of question was that, and what relevancy does it have on the case?*

"Around ten years. Does it make a difference?" Maria snapped.

"No. I was just wondering," Roberts mumbled.

"Why aren't you out there searching for the killer?"

"We are, we have teams gathering information on him now. As you can imagine, things will take a little time to piece together. He's a dangerous criminal and…" Charlie stated.

"And he's just gunned down my fiancée, and forgive me for saying this, but it's taken you over…" She glanced at the sunray-shaped clock on the wall. "I was wrong, it's more like fifteen or sixteen hours to get here. I rang the station, you know. They didn't want to know."

"What?" Roberts beat Charlie in saying. "Can you give me some details about that?"

"What else do I have to tell you? I was frantic. As soon as I heard the shots, I rang the station. Maybe I would've been better off calling nine-nine-nine. Hindsight is a wonderful thing."

"Can you tell me who you spoke to?"

"A young woman. I figured she would do something about it and get back to me. I've been sitting up all night, waiting for someone to drop by."

"We spoke to the parking attendant. The garage was locked around eight-thirty and remained closed until around eight this morning. In our defence, maybe a patrol car turned up at the location, found it locked and—"

"Are you serious?" Maria interrupted Roberts. "I've bloody heard it all now. My friends are always telling me the police are a waste of time, you guys have just proved it. Is it because of who we are? Because we're not straight we don't get the same treatment as straight folks? Tell me, I'd love to know."

Charlie sat back and let Roberts take over. This was way over her head.

"No, I don't think that's accurate at all. I promise to delve into your complaint when we get back to the station. All I can do for now is apologise for the way your emergency call was handled. It's a grave concern to me that we appeared to have failed you. Please, let us try and put that right for you."

"And how do you propose doing that?" Maria sneered.

"By capturing the killer and making sure he faces the justice he deserves. There is also a complaints procedure you can enter into, if that's the route you'd like to take."

"I might want to do that in the future, not right now. I need to grieve the loss of Andrea. She meant everything to me. We'd overcome a lot in our relationship, enough to know that we were right for each other, no matter what hurdles were erected in our path to happiness. I know that probably sounds sloppy, but it's fact. Being gay...well, I'm sure by now you can understand how difficult it still is in our society. Everyone in authority believes we have equal rights, but when it comes down to it, we have nothing. It's all a load of bollocks. Unless you're straight in this life, well, it's one huge struggle to get noticed and have a voice of your own."

"I can understand you thinking that way. I'll give you a card. When you're ready to talk, or make a complaint, you'll have my backing, I promise you."

Maria's eyes glistened with tears. "You'd do that for me?"

"I would. I'm on the side of justice and I believe you were seriously let down by the force today. I'll ensure this doesn't happen in the future. I know that's not going to help your situation but I'd like to do my bit for the future."

"Thank you. That's very kind of you. What will happen to the person who accepted my call and did nothing?"

"I'll make it a priority to find out who was responsible and punish them accordingly."

"I hate to get someone in trouble but...well, I can't thank you enough for this. It's something that should never have been allowed to have happened. I'm too numb with grief to be angry, I suppose that will come later. At the moment, I'm too overwhelmed by my loss."

"We totally understand," Charlie chipped in, eager to show her support to the injustice of the situation.

"Okay, we're going to leave you alone now. Are you sure you'll be all right?" Roberts rose to his feet.

Charlie couldn't believe how quickly he was leaving but stood also.

"I have a friend coming down from Liverpool to be with me. She should be here by midday."

"That's good to hear. Here's my card, don't hesitate to call me if you think there's anything we should know about the investigation. Again, you have my condolences for your loss, *and* my word that I'll look into what went wrong on your behalf ASAP."

She showed them to the front door. Charlie patted the dog on her way out.

"Thank you. Do your best to find the shit before he kills someone else and causes more pain in his wake."

"You have my word," Roberts replied.

Outside, Charlie was quiet on the way back to the car. Once they were inside the vehicle, she said, "Do you think that was right, to tell her about the complaints procedure? Shouldn't you be shielding the officer who screwed up?"

He tutted. "You really have a lot to learn about me, Charlie. I'm a fair man in every respect. If I believe someone has been let down by the very people who have sworn to protect the public, then I will do everything in my power to right that wrong and to make amends."

"What consequences will the officer face once you find her?"

"She'll be reprimanded, might even face a suspension for her lack of commitment to the job. What would you do if you were in my shoes?"

Charlie pondered the question, aware of who she was riding with. "Probably the same, truth be told. How does someone screw up like this? It beggars belief, if you ask me. Even a novice would know it was imperative to follow up on a shooting incident."

"Not only that, this case has been rife in the media, therefore, it should have been treated as a matter of urgency. Wait, talking of media, has Katy held a press conference yet?"

"No. She hasn't had the time. We've been going from one murder scene to the next with very little time in between to organise anything. Mind you, now that we know who the suspect is, do you think it would be a good idea to hold one?"

"I know she was wary of holding one, I'm overruling her, think it's a must. We need to flush him out. Let's face it, we don't have a clue where he is, do we?"

"True enough. Do you want me to arrange one when we return to base?" Charlie asked.

"Do you think you're up to the task?"

"Of organising one, yes, I can do that."

"What about chairing it?"

Charlie got the impression he was testing her, again. "Umm...I'm not sure I'm up to performing on the grand stage just yet. I could sit alongside you while you do it, though."

"Coward. Okay, we'll compromise, I'll chair it and you give out the details as you're more familiar with them. How does that sound to you?"

Charlie turned to face him, her mouth gaping open. Recovering, she replied, "Goodness me. You're really going to throw me to the lions this early on in my career?"

"My motto is to take the bull by the horns. You need to make adjustments quickly in this game, Charlie."

"You mean either sink or swim, don't you?"

"Maybe." He laughed and patted her on the knee. "Sorry, I got carried away, I shouldn't have touched you. I'll be there to back you up. Are you up for it?"

"Do I have a choice?"

"Nope."

Her heart rate escalated at the thought of sitting in front of a swarm of probing journalists. *Crap! How the hell am I going to handle this? I've been through worse in my life and come out the other end, kind of unscathed-ish. I've got this, it'll be a cinch compared to dealing with the Unicorn and what he put me through in my teens.*

. . .

*C*harlie managed to arrange a press conference for later that afternoon. Her nerves jangled throughout the day, but as soon as she entered the designated conference room, an unexplained calmness descended. Maybe the call she'd made to her mother ten minutes before had forced the change.

Lorne had told her how proud she was of her and insisted she go in there determined and full of confidence. If the journalists picked up on any hesitation on her part, they'd pounce and rip her to shreds. Two minutes before the 'kick off', DCI Roberts joined her at the table.

"How are you feeling?"

"Like you're throwing me to a pack of crazed wolves," she lied.

He chuckled. "I can tell when you're lying, Charlie."

"You can? I'm fine. I rang Mum, and she gave me a few pointers which helped me deal with my anxiety."

"Let's face it, you've been through far worse in the past."

"That's what she said. I know you're continually testing me. I hope I don't dry up and let you down."

"You could never let me down. Give me a nudge under the table if one of them asks a question you find too difficult to answer."

"I will, thank you."

"Let the show begin." He turned his attention to the crowd and asked them to settle down. "I'd like to introduce a new detective to you all, DC Charlie Simpkins. Unfortunately, her partner, DI Foster, is taking time off with family issues at present. DC Simpkins has been working alongside me in the interim. She'll run through why we've called this conference today. Be gentle with her."

Charlie smiled at Sean and cleared her throat. She professionally explained the details of the case, mentioning the four murders known to them and offered up a grainy picture they'd downloaded from the CCTV at Zedex. "This is James Boyd. He's a person of interest in the murders."

"You mean he's a main suspect, DC Simpkins? Any relation to former DI Lorne Simpkins by any chance?" one of the older journalists asked.

Charlie smiled at him and did her best to battle the heat rising in her cheeks. "I am. She's my mother and she taught me well."

The journalist nodded.

Roberts jumped in. "We're trying to find James Boyd and we're calling on the public to lend us a hand. Do you know him? Have you seen Boyd in the last forty-eight hours? Has he just moved to your area? Anything and everything you can tell us about this man will help at this stage."

"Why do you suspect his involvement in the investigation?" a female journalist asked.

Roberts took over again. "Primarily because he was a former employee at Zedex."

"So he's been bumping off his ex-colleagues? Do you know why?"

"His motive is unknown at present. We believe it's possibly to do with a recent promotion at Zedex. He has since left the firm and started up his own business in the same vein. We're eager to speak with him, if only to eliminate him from our enquiries."

"Really? To only eliminate him, not to haul him in and interrogate him about the murders?" one of the younger male journalists asked with all the eagerness of a ten-week-old puppy.

"No, our initial contact would be to have a chat with Mr Boyd, so, I repeat, if anyone either knows where he's staying at the moment, or if they've seen him walking in their neighbourhood, I'd like you to call the number on the bottom of your screen." Roberts ended the conference. Luckily, the journalists didn't feel the need to prolong Charlie's angst, either that or they were keen to get back to work and write up their pieces for the next day's newspapers.

"How do you feel now that's out of the way?" Roberts asked as they made their way back upstairs.

"Relieved. It actually went better than expected."

"I'd like to add that you're a natural in front of the camera. I know a certain person who is going to be exceptionally proud of your capabilities when she sees it."

Charlie glanced at him shyly. "I know it was your intention to throw me in at the deep end, maybe that's the way everyone should learn."

"I've always believed it to be the only way to learn. I'm not one for mollycoddling people, especially those with exceptional abilities to start with."

She placed a hand on her chest. "Moi?"

"Of course. I have every faith in you, Charlie, and I foresee you sitting behind my desk one day and going one step better than your mother." He shrugged. "Maybe even higher up the ladder than that. You've got your head screwed on and you were brought up by one of the best police officers ever to have worked for the Met. Those kinds of credentials have to count for something, right?"

"I hope I don't let you down. I never dreamed of being a copper, not from a young age. I suppose I was too rebellious until…well, you know what. After that, my outlook on life dramatically altered. Don't forget I had two generations of Met coppers at home. Granddad loved his time on the force and always regaled me with accounts on some of the major investigations he had under his belt." She fell quiet. Although she thought about her grandfather often, she didn't openly speak about him.

Roberts smiled. "Sam was an excellent copper. You come from the best stock around, Charlie, remember that when you're sitting at your desk doubting your ability during an investigation. I believe in you as a person, otherwise I wouldn't have invited you to join the team. Promise me one thing."

Charlie paused midway up the stairs. "What's that, sir?"

"You'll seek my help if ever you need it. If you don't, and your mother finds out that I haven't noticed you're struggling, she'll chop my testicles off and feed them to those damn dogs of hers."

Charlie laughed. "You're probably right."

"Okay, let's see what the team has to offer. Hopefully the phones will start ringing around mid-afternoon once the conference goes out. We'd better prepare ourselves for a late one. I wonder how Katy is getting on at the hospital."

"I thought about calling her but the last thing I want to do is cause her more anxiety."

"Yep, it's a tough one. Let's see what today brings, and maybe I'll be able to call her later with the good news that we've captured Boyd."

"Maybe. Do you think that's likely, sir?"

"You never know your luck."

They entered the incident room, and Graham immediately motioned for them to join him.

"I've been searching the ANPRs for the stolen cars and stumbled across this one, sir."

Charlie and Sean leaned in to the screen to get a closer look at the driver.

"I think that's him," Charlie confirmed. She opened the file she'd taken to the conference with her and held up the image they had of Boyd.

All three of them agreed.

"This is good news," Roberts insisted.

"Yeah, all we have to do now is find the car," Charlie replied, sensing they had a major task on their hands.

"Another thought struck me while you were both at the conference," Graham said.

"Go on," Roberts urged.

"What about the other two, the only two colleagues left at Zedex? Do you think we should keep them under surveillance or some form of protection?"

Charlie nodded. "It has to be done. He could strike at any moment. Do we know if the two men are still at work?"

"Do you want me to call them?" Karen volunteered.

Roberts spun around to look at her. "Yes, do it."

Karen picked up the phone and dialled the number. She spoke to someone who answered and nodded. "Okay, we'll get back to you soon." She ended the call and told them, "Yes, they're both there. Totally shaken up by what's happened to Andrea today. Unsure what to do, whether they should stay at work or go home."

"Understandable, any suggestions?" Roberts asked.

"It would be better to keep them in one place. Maybe we could send a couple of uniformed officers over there, make sure no one enters the building who could put them in jeopardy," Charlie suggested.

"I think you're right. Can you arrange that with the desk sergeant, Charlie?"

"On it now." Charlie raced over to her desk and contacted Mick who promised to send two men out to Zedex immediately.

Roberts seemed thoughtful upon her return.

"Everything all right, sir?" she asked.

"Yes, sort of. Recalling what Maria said about when she'd placed the call. I need to look into that, make sure we're not dealing with anything more sinister than we first thought."

Charlie gasped. "Someone on the inside?"

"Why not? We're talking guns again. You know what happened regarding another recent case where a gun was used. I need to get on to Patti or Forensics to see what they've come up with, if anything."

"God, I hope you're wrong."

"So do I. I'll be right back." He headed into Katy's office. "A coffee would be most welcome," he threw over his shoulder on the way.

"Coming right up."

He disappeared into the office and closed the door.

"Shit! He never bloody puts his hand in his pocket. I'm going to be broke by the end of the ruddy week at this rate."

Graham dug into his pocket and slapped a handful of change onto the desk. "There you go, it shouldn't always fall on your shoulders, Charlie."

Charlie pinched his cheek. "You're a gent." She slotted the coins into the vending machine and took the coffee in to Roberts. One look at his face, and she could tell he was livid. Charlie tried to retreat, but he gestured for her to take a seat. She sat there for the next five minutes squirming on behalf of the person receiving a bollocking on the other end of the line.

Roberts hung up and sat back. He blew out an exasperated breath.

"What the fuck! I've heard some trivial excuses in my time on the force, but that has to be right up there with the worst of them. Why can't every new recruit be as enthusiastic about their role as you are? To some of them it would seem that getting a monthly salary for sitting behind a damn desk all day is the answer to their problems."

"I'm sure that's not true, although it might appear to be the case, sir."

"Well, she's got an official warning coming her way. I refuse to put up with that sort of tardiness, not on my watch."

"Sorry it happened, sir."

"So am I. Thanks for the drink. I feel a lot calmer now than I did a few minutes ago. My one bugbear doing this job is dealing with ineptness. There's no bloody need for it, is there? We're talking about supposedly intelligent people here, aren't we? What's your opinion on the new crop of recruits we've been laden with this year?"

"Gosh, I'd rather you didn't put me on the spot like that, sir."

"May I ask why?"

Why? Because you're asking me to spy or tell tales on my fellow officers. How do you think that's going to make me look? She couldn't help feeling torn. Damned if she answered him truthfully and damned if she let things ride. "I didn't see any problems during my training assignments, sir."

He narrowed his eyes and tilted his head. "You wouldn't be trying to pull a fast one on me, Simpkins, would you?"

"No, sir. It was a genuine answer. You know me, I prefer to keep to myself, knuckle down and get the job done." She hoped her answer would appease him. If not, she didn't know which way she should turn next.

"Okay, whilst I admire your loyalty, I would hope that if you saw anything not quite right in the system, you would let me know."

"That goes without saying, sir. I promise you." Charlie's phone rang. Embarrassed, she glanced at the caller ID, willing it not to be Brandon. It wasn't, it was Katy. "Can I take this, it's Katy?"

"Stay there, put it on speaker, if you would?"

And what if Katy didn't appreciate me doing that?

"Hi, Katy, you're on speaker. I'm with DCI Roberts."

"Oh, of course. I'm sorry, have I called at an inappropriate time?"

"Not at all, Katy. How's Georgie?" Roberts jumped in.

"The signs are good. They've said they'll be keeping her in for the next week or so. Before you say it, AJ and I have spoken about this, and we've agreed that I should return to work tomorrow."

"Are you sure?" Charlie asked. Putting herself in Katy's position, she'd want to remain at the hospital with her child until the danger had passed at least.

"I echo what Charlie just said. We're fine at this end, don't go rushing back if things are still fraught at the hospital."

"I'm getting the impression that I'm not wanted there." Katy sounded subdued.

"Don't be silly," Charlie was quick to add. "All we're saying is take care of Georgie's needs first."

"I know you both care, but I think it's for the best. AJ is fed up with having me under his feet, or he will be by the end of the day. The medical staff are keeping her sedated for now, allowing her body to heal itself without putting extra strain on her heart. It seems to be working. The rash is still prominent in some areas but has vanished in others. The nursing staff told me it varies from patient to patient. Here's hoping she's over the worst of it."

"Sounds good, a steady progress anyway." Relief flooded through Charlie.

"So, don't keep me in suspense, what's going on there?"

"Nothing much." Charlie tried to keep the investigation advancement to a minimum on purpose, but Roberts had other ideas and opened his big mouth.

"Charlie held a press conference."

"Wow, go you, Charlie. How did it go?"

"It went exceedingly well," Roberts added before Charlie had a chance to answer for herself.

"We're just waiting on the results from that. I was a tad nervous but not as bad as I thought I was going to be," Charlie said after clearing her throat.

"Great news. You can take over doing them once you become DS, I hate the damn things. Talking of which, that's another reason I'll be coming back to work tomorrow, so you can toodle off to your exam."

"Hey, don't leave your sick child on my account. I can easily postpone it for a few weeks."

"Phooey! You're going, end of."

"You're a star, Katy. Hopefully, if I get through the exam I'll be even more of an asset to the team." She glanced up, and Roberts shook his head. She frowned and mouthed, "What?"

"Are you going to say it, Sean, or do I need to?" Katy said.

"My take is, that young Simpkins here is fishing for compliments." They all laughed.

"No seriously," Charlie chimed in. "I truly mean it. I never want to be a burden, so you must tell me if I ever become one."

"Blah, blah, blah...what a lot of nonsense you speak, young lady," Katy admonished good-naturedly.

"Umm...joking aside, we have news for you." Charlie cringed when Roberts shook his head.

"Oh, what's that?"

"There's been another murder. It took place in the Zedex underground car park," Charlie said.

"Oh bugger. Who?"

Charlie sighed. "Andrea Gregory."

"Fuck," Katy muttered. "What about the other two colleagues?"

"We've got that sorted, don't worry. Just concentrate on looking after Georgie for now," Roberts said.

"All right. You've clearly got everything under control there, I'll leave you to it. No, wait, any sightings on Boyd yet?"

"Not yet, except we think we spotted him driving one of the stolen vehicles we highlighted yesterday. Graham is tracking the vehicle on the ANPR cameras now."

"That is good news. Keep a close eye on him, he's likely to dump the car again. Get the desk sergeant to make sure his staff are out there searching for it and any possible dumpings in the meantime."

"Go. It's in hand, we promise. Thanks for keeping us updated, Katy. Love to AJ," Charlie said.

"Good luck tomorrow in the exam, Charlie. Fingers and toes crossed for you, not that you'll need it."

"I appreciate it. Speak soon." Charlie ended the call.

"Good news. Let's hope we can keep the momentum going and receive the news we want from the appeal when it goes out."

Charlie rose from her seat. "I'll get back and share the good news with the team, sir, leave you to get on with your paperwork."

"Be sure to give me a shout if anything interesting crops up. I can drop all of this in an instant."

Charlie left the room. "Katy's just rung. Looks like Georgie is on the mend, although it's very early days yet. She'll be back at work tomorrow. I tried to persuade her otherwise, but she's adamant she wants to get back. Also, she's aware I won't be here tomorrow because of the dreaded exam I have to attend."

"You'll be fine," Patrick called out.

The others added their encouragement, too, which lifted her.

"You guys are the best. I wish I had your faith. How's it going, Graham?"

"I followed the car through to Whitechapel and then lost it."

Charlie's high came crashing down. "Damn. All we can hope now is that a member of the public living in that area calls in and gives us a possible address."

The team's frustrations mounted during the course of the day because the phones remained silent until gone five-thirty when Charlie took an interesting call from a resident around the Whitechapel area. It was too much of a coincidence to ignore the call, given what Graham had spotted on the cameras earlier that day.

"Yes, Mrs Smallwood, any information you can give us about James Boyd will go a long way to help our investigation."

"Good, good, umm…not that I can really tell you much. I've seen him in my street a few times. Croft Road, it is, dear. You'll need to look it up on the map, I'm in my seventies and not one for giving accurate directions, I'm afraid. And hubby is long gone, so I can't even hand the phone over to someone else to fill you in either."

"Don't worry, I can sort that out. Can I ask if the gentleman in question visited a certain house at all?"

"I couldn't tell you that. He walked past my window one day, looking over his shoulder and acting suspiciously, which drew my attention. Then he got in a blue car. I know what you're going to say next, no, I neither know the make nor model of it. I'm sorry to be so useless."

"Goodness me, you're far from that, believe me. Your call could be just what we've been waiting for to solve this case."

"Really? I saw you on the TV, and I've been sitting here debating whether to ring you or not, thought I'd be wasting your time. What with me not knowing much."

"Nonsense. We appreciate your call. We haven't had many and were beginning to get concerned."

"Oh, in that case, I'm glad I took the plunge."

"If I can just take your details for our records. We'll look into the information you've given us."

Mrs Smallwood gave her address and phone number and added, "I hope this doesn't come back and bite me in the bum. I'm all for helping folks out but I've never snitched to the police before. That is the right term, isn't it?"

"It is. Although, I wouldn't class what you've just told me as snitching. I can't thank you enough for contacting us. Promise me you'll stay vigilant, and if you should see this man in your area in the near future, will you call us?"

"Oh, I will that. I thought I'd be nervous speaking to an officer of the law, but I must say, you have a nice way about you, my dear."

"Thank you. I do my best. Enjoy your evening, Mrs Smallwood."

"I'll do that now I've relieved myself of such a burden. Thank you and good luck."

Charlie ended the call and left her desk. "Graham, I've taken an interesting call from a sweet old lady."

"Is there any other type? Oh, wait, I take that back. I remember what my foul-mouthed gran used to be like. Sorry, I digress, you were saying, Charlie?"

She smiled and shook her head. "You're nuts. Anyway, adding to what we learnt earlier, about the car disappearing in the Whitechapel area, she lives in Croft Road. Can you bring it up on the map, see how close it is to where the car went missing?"

He tapped a few keys and zoomed in on the map. "Croft Road, ah, here it is. Yeah, it's not far, not far at all, in fact."

"I'm going to run it past DCI Roberts."

At that moment, he chose to come out of the office and caught the tail end of their conversation. "What's that?"

Charlie ran through what they'd uncovered. "What do you think we should do now, sir, bearing in mind the restrictions we have in place?"

"Hogwash. We forget about them for the time being. We've got a serial killer on the loose, and it's imperative we bring the shit down. Let's get some patrol cars doing what they do best in the area and see what that brings."

Charlie grimaced and then tutted. "What if he's changed his car by now?"

Roberts groaned. "Then we're up the proverbial creek, aren't we? Get the patrol cars organised, Charlie. Then I think we should call it a day."

Charlie's eyes were drawn to the clock on the wall.

"Something wrong, DC Simpkins?" Roberts followed her gaze.

"Umm...no, sir. I was wondering what the time was, that's all. Gosh, is it that late already? Doesn't time fly when—?"

"Yes, yes. It may only be five-forty, but I think we should go home all the same."

Graham glanced at Charlie. She saw him turn his head her way, but her focus remained on Roberts.

"What is it, Graham?" DCI Roberts demanded. "I'm getting the distinct impression that none of you have homes to go to, am I wrong?"

"It's just that..." Graham started and stopped.

"It's just that we need to be around to man the phones, sir, you know, what with the press conference going out on the evening news," Charlie finished off for her colleague who seemed relieved at her interjection.

"Oh yes. You're right. Well, in my eyes it's only going to need one person to remain behind, and only for a maximum of two hours. Who's up for the job?"

Charlie grinned. "I'll happily volunteer, sir."

"What utter nonsense. You have swatting up to do this evening for your important exam tomorrow, or had you forgotten about that, Simpkins?"

"Hardly, sir. I could do all my revision here, while I answer the calls."

He blew out a breath. "Very well, if that's how you want to go about things, who am I to argue with you? The rest of you can pack up and go home."

He left the incident room before anyone else could argue the toss with him.

As soon as the door closed behind him, Patrick whispered, "Is he for real? We're closing in on a serial killer, and he wants us to put the brakes on and piss off home. What the fuck?"

Charlie shook her head. "It's the cuts driving his decision, I'm sure it is. You guys go, leave me to man the phones."

Karen shook her head. "That's not fair on you, Charlie. You've got important revision to do this evening. Let me stay here and you go home."

"Honestly, I'm fine. Don't worry about me, I wasn't planning on revising that much anyway to tell you the truth. I'll hang around until eight as instructed and then call it a day."

The team despondently switched off their equipment, and reluctantly left her to it.

Charlie found the empty incident room eerie to begin with. She shuddered as a cool breeze swept past her half an hour later. She shot out of her chair, a prominent thought in her mind. She glanced at the door, making sure it was shut and asked, "Pete, is that you?" She recollected the stories her mother used to tell her regarding her former partner always being present. She sniffed the air. A faint smell of after-shave wafted under her nose, and she knew he was close by. She'd regarded Pete as an uncle figure when she was younger, he'd been a good man. Why was he here? To protect her? Or had he come to take her with him?

She shook the ghastly thought from her head. *No, not the latter, please, not that!*

The faintest of laughs spooked her. *Is he reading my mind? Can spirits do that? Where's Carol when I need her?*

Charlie flipped open her revision folder and concentrated on that, instead of trying to figure out things that were beyond her.

Just like that, Pete seemed to disappear. The phone on her desk rang, and she almost leapt out of her seat. "DC Simpkins, how can I help?"

The caller was one of those nuisance calls she'd heard so much about. The young man ended the conversation with a laugh and hung up, leaving her frustrated as she crossed through the information he'd spent five minutes giving her.

"Fucking dipshit!" The rest of the evening proved to be a disap-pointment. Maybe the chief was right in his thinking, ordering the staff to go home early. She packed up at around eight and left the station.

Now all she had to do was go home, rustle up some dinner and get a good night's sleep. She had a feeling sleep wouldn't be on the agenda, not with her mind whirling up a storm before her exam.

---

9

*B*oyd was on the prowl again. He'd followed the two men to the pub. Laughed when he saw the two uniformed coppers get out of their car and take up their positions on either side of the main entrance.

"The guys always did like their drink. Fancy dragging the coppers along with them. What a waste of police time."

What are you going to do? Sit here and wait for them to come out?

"What other option do I have? I can't go in there and do the deed, can I?"

It sucks either way. It's a cold December evening, we should be tucked up at home in front of a roaring open fire.

"You do talk a load of shit at times. That squat is colder than the damn car. I can't wait for all this to be over and to get back to the house. It might not be much, but at least it was comfortable."

Fecking idiot, as if you'll be able to go back there after what you've done!

"Correction, what *we've* done. You're just as responsible as me. In fact, you're the one who drove me to kill the others. All I wanted to do was have some fun, for them to regret their actions."

Where would the fun *have been in that? Glad to see you've finally grown a pair. Shame you didn't kill Dad sooner, while we're on the subject of growing a pair.*

"He got what was coming to him in the end. I was biding my time. I needed to make it look convincing. Poisoning him was the only plausible way I could think of to get rid of the old bastard."

It wasn't good enough. If I'd had my way, he would have been kept in an underground storage unit and tortured to within an inch of his life every goddamn day after what he did. Sticking his dick up your arse like that. Fucking sick shit.

Boyd swallowed down the acid burning his throat. "Did you have to remind me of that? Why do you do it? Why can't you leave things alone?"

Furthermore, you should have cut it off and forced him to eat that vile wrinkled sausage of his.

"Enough, I don't want to think about him. He got what was due to him. Why do you have to keep raising the subject all the time?"

Because I like to poke you with a stick. Not a dick like he used to, no, a stick. You need to get rid of your softer side and start treating people the way they should be treated. The way they treat you. Disrespectfully. What your colleagues did to you was nothing more than a disgrace.

"Don't you think I know that? Which is why I've set out on this reckless path. To punish those who felt it right to treat me like an idiot. To ditch me in favour of that bitch despite my success record and years of experience. Well, I showed them, didn't I?"

Sort of. You still have these two to see to and then you can go off and live life to the fullest again. Whores and drink and debauchery, I think that should be in your future. I'm up for it anyway.

Boyd laughed. "Does anyone say debauchery these days? You're crazy. No, I want the opposite. I'll sell everything. If the coppers won't allow me to do that, then I'll leave the house and take off."

And live on what? You clearly haven't thought things through, as usual.

"Then I'll rob a bank or swindle some money out of an investor. Yes, that's what I'll do."

Now you're talking!

His inner voice died down, and he rested his head back, his gaze fixed on the front door. An hour later, he saw one of the coppers reach for his mobile. Was that a signal? He snatched up his rifle and took up his position from the rear of the car park. He'd specifically chosen this spot, far enough away that the coppers wouldn't detect him and close enough to be within range to take the shot and drive away before they had a chance to know what hit them. Excitement mixed with fear coursed through his veins. He peered through the sniper scope and placed his finger on the trigger. The coppers glanced over their shoulders, one facing the pub and the other facing the car park. There was definite movement up ahead.

The second Ben and Steve emerged, his hand shook.

Don't you dare back down, not after you've come so far.

"I won't. Shut the fuck up and let me concentrate."

The coppers walked them back to the vehicle, one on either side of the two men. Boyd fired off two quick rounds. Ben immediately dropped to the ground. The coppers tried to shield Steve, but it was too late. Boyd took aim a second time and fired off another couple of shots. The coppers lay on the ground, their bodies flung across the two men. He started the car, purposefully kept the lights off and drove quietly out of the car park, keeping to the rear of the other parked vehicles. It wasn't until he reached the main road that he switched on the lights and floored the accelerator.

He drove a few feet then steered the car into an alley he'd spotted earlier and, turning in his seat, he watched three patrol cars whizz past him, their sirens wailing like crazed cats and their blue lights illuminating the dense night surrounding him. He remained in the same location for the next twenty minutes and then slipped onto the main road again and headed back to the squat. A few roads away, he decided it would be best to dump the car and steal another one. Was he taking a risk doing it in his own backyard?

Boyd was past caring. He wouldn't be sticking around here much longer anyway, now that everyone had been dealt with.

---

10

*C*harlie had just arrived home when the desk sergeant rang her. "Hi, yes, I can attend. Give me the address. Were the officers injured?"

"No, they escaped injury. Sorry my guys let you down, or should I say, the victims down."

"He's a determined killer, your guys were lucky not to get harmed. What were they doing in the pub?"

"The men insisted they needed a drink to calm their nerves."

"Jesus, what is wrong with people? Okay, I'm on my way. Crap, I have a dilemma now, who should I call for assistance, DI Foster or DCI Roberts?"

"I didn't know either, hence the reason I called you," Mick confessed.

"Leave it with me. I'll call Roberts, see what he says." Charlie disconnected and immediately rang Roberts. "Hi, I'm very sorry to disturb you, sir, but I have a quandary."

"Charlie, do you realise what the time is?"

"I do, which is why I apologised about disturbing you. The thing is, there's been another shooting."

"What? Where? And yes, you've done the right thing getting in touch with me. Why the hesitation?"

"I wasn't sure if you'd handed the reins over to Katy or not yet."

"No, that'll happen in the morning."

"I see. I'm on my way to the crime scene."

"Where?"

"Outside a pub, the Wheatsheaf on Saunders Road. Do you know it?"

"As it happens, I do. I'll meet you there." Roberts ended the call.

Charlie raced upstairs to get changed and came back down to Brandon waiting for her at the front door. He was holding her coat out for her. She slipped her arms into it and kissed him. "I'm so sorry to be running out on you, again."

"Charlie, don't be, it goes with the job, right? I understand that. Do you think it'll get any easier once you're a sergeant?"

She pulled on one ankle boot and then the other and kissed him again. "I doubt it, it'll probably be a darn sight worse, knowing my luck."

His face dropped. "In that case, I think we'll need to sit down and have a proper chat about our future at the weekend."

"What? You're dumping this on me now? When I have to attend another murder scene? Okay, we'll talk soon. Just remember one thing, Brandon, before you think about calling off our engagement."

"What's that?"

"I love you. I might not always show it but I regard you as my rock. There, I've said it." She pecked him on the lips and rushed out of the front door. Glancing over the roof of the car, she saw him hesitate for a few seconds before he went back inside.

She tried to set aside her personal problems and concentrated on her driving instead. She failed, and her thoughts turned to her mother's situation and how she had coped all those years being married to her father. She hadn't realised at the time how much of a bastard he'd been to her. Brandon wasn't from the same mould as her father, he was a much more placid person. She hoped they could get past this sticky patch. If not, she'd focus on her career for the next ten years and see where that led her. Easy come, easy go, life was too short to be down-hearted all the time.

Arriving at the scene, she sought out DCI Roberts who was already organising the uniform team to guard the pub, ensuring the punters remained inside rather than gawping at the victims.

"I'm here at last, sir. Sorry for the delay, traffic!"

"It doesn't matter. The good news is that we're dealing with one victim. Ben Thompson has been whisked off to hospital with life-threatening wounds."

"Damn. Sorry one of them didn't make it."

"Can you collaborate with the pathologist—not sure I have anything to say to her at present—while I continue barking out the orders and coordinating the taking down of statements?"

"Leave it with me." Charlie went in search of Patti.

"We meet again, and so soon." Patti rolled her eyes. "I take it the victim, and the one who was taken to hospital, both worked at Zedex?"

"They did. They're the last known colleagues of the murderer. The question is, what is he going to do next?"

"Who bloody knows if he can take two people out under the noses of uniformed coppers?"

"That was my thinking. This is over my head." Charlie kicked out at a stone close to her foot and sent it hurtling towards a car a few feet away. It hit the metal wheel trim and *tinged*.

Patti tapped her upper arm with a fisted hand. "Hey, you can pack that in. Don't go taking this personally. I'll let you in on a secret."

Charlie's brow furrowed. "I'm listening."

Patti crossed her arms, her paper suit rustling. She lowered her voice so only Charlie could hear. "It's beyond me, too. I mean, we all get ticked off at work from time to time, but how many of us go around killing off any colleagues who have wronged us? The answer is not many, not from what I've seen anyway."

"By that, what you're saying is that there's something far more sinister going on than just a falling out with ex-colleagues."

Patti tapped her forefinger against her temple and nodded. "Up here."

"Mental problems? Wait, yes, I see. One of the victims, Rufus, he wasn't a colleague at all, was he? I get it."

"Yep. What you've got to hope for now is that he doesn't start delving deeper into who has pissed him off over the years. Hopefully, he'll settle on the damage he's already caused and decide to call it quits."

"God! Can you bloody imagine the death toll if he took that into consideration?" Charlie groaned.

"Nope, it's too mind-blowing to consider."

Roberts joined them. "Ladies, have we established anything yet?"

"Lots," Charlie replied.

"Good. You can fill me in on the way to the victims' addresses." He sighed heavily and mumbled as he walked away. "Not something I'm bloody relishing, I can tell you. Chop-chop, Charlie." He sniggered. "I like that, it could become your nickname."

Charlie grimaced and widened her eyes at Patti who was shaking her head and pulling a weird expression. "I bloody hope not," Charlie muttered.

She took off after Roberts.

Charlie caught up with him at his car. "We've got two cars. Wouldn't it make sense to tackle the families separately? I could go to Ben's home, it'll be less of a chore for me, dealing with a family who has hope he'll survive."

"You're suggesting I go break the news to Abbot's family, is that it?"

Charlie nodded.

"You're smarter than you think, DC Simpkins. You're right, it does make sense. Even though I would prefer you being with me, you know, to offer backup at a stressful time. If we go our separate ways we'll get things accomplished much faster and we'll be able to get home sooner."

That's not what Charlie was thinking, but if that's what he wanted to believe, who was she to argue with him? "Yes, sir."

"You're aware of the victims' addresses, I take it?"

"Yes, Patti has them."

"Nip back and get them, and then we can proceed."

Charlie trotted back to Patti and collected the information then returned to the car. She tore a sheet of paper from her notebook and handed it to Roberts. "Abbot's address, sir."

"Thanks. I'll tell the victim's family the state of play and then head home. Good luck tomorrow with your exam."

Charlie was stunned at his blasé approach and the lack of emotion evident in his expression, which ticked her off for some reason. Her own stomach was tied in knots at the thought of telling the victim's family what had occurred; however, she was more worried about his attitude when he reached his destination. "Thank you, sir. Are you sure you're...?"

"What? Up to this? I'm sure. It won't be easy, but it's got to be done. Goodnight." He jumped into his vehicle, started the engine, and the gravel scattered in every direction as he drove out of the car park.

"Are you all right, Charlie?" Patti asked, coming up behind her.

"Yeah, just gobsmacked. Ignore me. Give me working alongside Katy any goddamn day of the week."

"Any news on that front? Not wishing to hold you up, but I'm eager to know how her daughter is faring."

"Katy's back at work tomorrow. Georgie appears to have turned the corner, for now."

"What a relief. I hope the little one makes a full recovery, it's a vile disease to recover from."

"I know. I believe my granddad caught it not long before his death. It weakened him terribly."

"Does anyone else know that?"

Charlie dipped her head. "No, I didn't deem it necessary for them to know. Maybe Katy knew and just forgot, I don't know."

"You poor thing. Do you need a hug?"

Charlie smiled and raised a hand. "Nope. I have work today. Personal emotions need to be set aside for now."

"You're an amazing young woman, no wonder you have the proudest mother walking this earth."

"Get away with you. See you soon—not too soon, though, I hope."

Charlie hopped behind the steering wheel, waved at Patti and entered the details in the satnav before she left the car park. She arrived at the Thompsons' house around five minutes later, meaning the Wheatsheaf must have been his local. She inhaled and exhaled a few deep breaths and left the car.

The exterior of the house was lit up with numerous strands of Christmas lights, and there was a five-foot plastic snowman in the centre of the front lawn. It brought home to her what this time of year meant: it was supposed to be about bringing joy and peace on earth, and here she was, about to tell the victim's family he'd been rushed to hospital after being shot. *Life can be shitty as hell some days!*

She rang the bell.

A dark-haired woman with a welcoming face greeted her. "Hello, can I help?" She glanced past Charlie as if she was expecting someone else.

"Mrs Thompson?"

Her expression changed to one of concern. "I am. Jo Thompson, and you are?"

Charlie presented her ID. "DC Simpkins. Would it be okay if we went inside?"

"Oh no. This is about Ben, isn't it? I've been expecting him home for the last half an hour, he's never late. I tried calling his mobile, but it was off. Please, tell me he's okay."

"Inside, if possible, Jo. May I call you Jo?"

"Yes, yes, come in. Of course you can. Come through to the lounge." She raced to stand by the mantelpiece and placed her elbow on it for support. "What's wrong?"

Charlie chose to stand while she delivered the news. "I'm sorry to have to inform you that your husband was injured tonight as he left the pub. He's on his way to the hospital now."

"What? Has someone attacked him? I don't understand."

"No, it was a shooting."

"No!" she screamed.

"Please, won't you take a seat? Can I get you a glass of water? Is there someone I can call to be with you?"

"Yes, my mother. I need her here with me. Oh God, is he badly hurt?"

"First things first. Do you have your mother's number?"

She snatched her phone off the coffee table and punched in a number then handed it to Charlie. "Her name is Sue."

"Hi, Jo, I was just thinking about ringing you, everything all right?"

"Hello, Sue. I'm DC Simpkins, I'm here at Jo's house. She's asked me to call you to see if you would come and join us."

"What? You're not making any sense. Police? Why are you there? Has she done something wrong?"

"Just listen, Mum," Jo shouted, annoyed.

"All right. I'm listening. I'm not coming until you tell me what's going on."

Charlie sighed. "Your son-in-law was involved in an incident tonight. He's on his way to the hospital to receive treatment. Jo wondered if you wouldn't mind coming to be with her."

"Why didn't you say that in the first place? Oh my…I'll be there in five minutes. Where the hell did I put my car keys? Oh God, poor Ben. I'm coming, sweetheart. Mummy is on her way."

Jo shook her head and grabbed the phone out of Charlie's hand. "Maybe I should have called her later. She'll be faffing around now."

"Sorry. Do you want to take a seat until she gets here? I'll accompany you to the hospital."

"How bad is he? He was with his work colleague, Steve. Was he hurt in the attack?"

Charlie chewed her lip and shook her head. "Sorry, Steve was shot also, but he didn't survive."

"Oh God, poor Valerie. No, I can't believe this is happening. Why them? Has this got something to do with the other shootings? Stupid question, of course it has. Wait a minute, didn't I see you on the TV earlier, asking for the public's help?"

"You did. We're aware of who the killer is, we're in the process of trying to track him down. We had your husband under surveillance, two police officers were with him at the time."

"What? Are you telling me you've got the bastard or that you've let him go?"

"He used a sniper rifle to carry out the shootings. His only targets appeared to be your husband and Steve Abbott."

"Why? My husband isn't the type to fall out with people. Why is Boyd doing this?"

"We've yet to uncover a plausible motive. We've got a possible idea that it might be because of the promotion which he was overlooked for."

"Really? People take umbrage at something as silly as that?"

"We won't know the truth until we bring him in for questioning."

The front door opened, and a grey-haired woman wearing leggings and a long fluffy grey jumper burst into the room and smothered Jo. "My darling, it's such terrible news. Is he okay?"

"I'm just questioning the officer now, Mum, be patient."

"I'm afraid I can't answer your question," Charlie said. "What I can do is either take, or accompany you, to the hospital. Which do you prefer?"

"I'd rather go in my car, you know I don't trust other people driving me," Sue was quick to reply.

"She's right. She's a nightmare, you'd be a nervous wreck after having her as a passenger. You'll come with us? Be there with us at the hospital?"

"Yes. All right, I suggest we go now in that case."

The three of them headed out of the house. In the hallway, on the half-moon-shaped console table was a framed photo of Jo and Ben. Jo threw her coat on and then ran her hand over her husband's face in the photo.

A lump appeared in Charlie's throat that she cleared with a subtle cough on the way out to the car. "It shouldn't take us too long. Try and stick close behind me if you can. If I lose you, I'll pull over to allow you to catch up. We have a number of traffic lights to contend with on the way."

"I'll keep up, don't worry. It's not like a jobsworth copper is going to pull me over, is it?" Sue pointed out.

Charlie couldn't argue with her logic. The three women set off in their respective cars, and before long they were within spitting distance of the hospital. Charlie's phone rang. She glanced down at the caller ID. It was Katy.

"Hi, I'm driving."

"Sorry, want me to call you back?"

"No, I just wanted you to be aware in case I lost my signal. How are things?"

"I'm heading home for the night, leaving hospital now. Things seem to be going okay with Georgie. The doctor is pleased with her progress, which is a blessing. Why are you in the car and not tucked up at home revising?"

"I was at home. I got called out. You don't want to hear."

"You're wrong. What's going on, Charlie? I order you to tell me. There, I've said it!"

Charlie sniggered. "Briefly, because the hospital entrance is up ahead. Ben Thompson and Steve Abbott were both shot tonight. Abbott didn't make it, but I'm on the way to the hospital now, taking Ben's wife and mother-in-law with me, and no, they're not in the car before you ask."

"Shit, what a bummer. Hey, I caught you on TV on the early evening news. You did good, girl."

"Thanks. Roberts forced me into a corner. Now I feel guilty. Did I push Boyd into going after Ben and Steve?"

"Like hell! Don't even go there. Boyd has got an agenda, he won't stop until he's fulfilled it. Let's face it, there's no one left now, is there?"

"Ben, if he survives. What if he calls the hospital to check how he is and then shows up to finish the job?"

"Crikey! There's every possibility he'd do that. You need to put Ben under guard at the hospital."

"Already tried that. Both Ben and Steve were being accompanied by uniform when they got shot earlier. It wasn't a deterrent for Boyd, far from it."

"You're going to have to make the call, put an armed officer on the door if necessary, love."

"I was wondering about that. I'll run it past Roberts."

Katy tutted. "Where is he? He should be out there with you."

"He is, well, sort of. He's gone to break the bad news to Abbott's wife. Get this, then he's going to head home."

"Whoa! That's the last time you and I pull an all-nighter in the future then. What a...never mind. I'll sort it out with him in the morning. Did you get anything from the press conference?"

"A lady rang in telling me that she'd seen Boyd in Croft Road close to where we last spotted his latest stolen car."

"Excellent news. All right, I'll let you get on. Send me a text later, let me know how you get on at the hospital."

"Will do."

"And Charlie, good luck for tomorrow. You've got this."

"Thanks, Katy."

Charlie ended the call and found a parking spot. She waited outside her vehicle for Sue to go back and forth in the place she'd found, only to leave the space and park in a different one a little farther away. *Oh God, she'd do my head in! Come on, woman!*

She pinned a smile in place as Jo and Sue joined her. "We can go straight in, we'll pick the ticket up when we leave."

They raced through to the Accident and Emergency department, and Charlie asked at the reception desk if it would be possible for them to see the doctor treating Ben Thompson.

"Can I ask you to wait in the family room? It's over there, on the right. I'll see what I can find out after I've dealt with the queue."

"Of course." Charlie led the way.

The three of them took a seat. Sue flicked frantically through a magazine, not bothering to read any of the articles, while Jo and Charlie were lost in their own thoughts. Charlie was unsure what to say for the best.

Fifteen minutes later, the doctor came to see them. "Ben Thompson's family, I presume?"

Charlie introduced them all. "His wife and mother-in-law, I'm DC Simpkins. How is he, Doctor?"

"Honest truth? Very poorly. We've been forced to resuscitate him several times already. I believe we've got him stable, for now. I'm sorry to tell you this, but I think you should prepare yourselves for the worst."

"What? Why? What injuries does he have?" Jo clutched her mother's hand.

"We're sending him down to the theatre. X-rays show he has a bullet lodged close to his heart. It will need to be removed before we can assess him further. It's going to be a tough operation."

"How long will the operation take, Doctor?" Charlie asked.

"Could be an hour, it might even be six or eight. There's no telling until we open him up and see the damage that has been caused. I need to go now."

Charlie nodded. "Thank you for keeping us informed. Please, do your best for him."

"Of course. Once he's been operated on, I'll get someone to come and advise you of the outcome."

After he left, they all stared at each other. Jo was the first to crack, her strong resolve crumbling. Sue comforted her, and Charlie went in search of coffee.

She returned with three cups and distributed them. "Please, you need to have faith in the surgeon. It's the only way you're going to get through this, Jo."

"I know. It's the thought of him lying there, all alone. None of this makes sense."

Sue pointed at Charlie. "You shouldn't be here, you should be out there trying to find him."

Charlie couldn't argue, Sue was right. That wasn't how Roberts wanted to play this, though, so her hands were tied.

Another couple of hours dragged by until the doctor returned to share the news. "They've successfully removed the bullet. He's on his way to intensive care. You're welcome to visit him now."

"Thank you, Doctor, that's good news," Charlie replied on behalf of Jo and Sue who were hugging each other tightly.

Charlie's mind whirled. If Ben was on his way to ICU, he needed to have a guard placed outside. She decided to call Roberts from the hallway.

He barked a hello down the phone.

"Sorry to disturb you, sir, it's Charlie."

"I'm aware of that. Are you at home?"

"No, at the hospital still. Ben's had surgery to remove a bullet close to his heart. I was wondering if we could put an armed guard on his door, sir, in light of what has already happened this evening."

"Oh, you were, were you? No can do. A uniformed officer will suffice. Get it organised with the desk sergeant."

"As you wish. Sorry to bother you, sir." Charlie ended the call and stared at the damn phone. It appeared to heat up in her hand the longer she stared at it. *What the fuck! This is so wrong.*

Her mind made up, she didn't bother ringing the station. Instead, she led the ladies up to ICU and sat outside the unit for the rest of the night. No one would get past her, she was adamant about that.

11

*K*aty got on the road early that morning, eager to get to work and see how the investigation had progressed overnight. She'd received a text at around eleven from Charlie, telling her she would remain at the hospital to ensure that Ben stayed safe, in case Boyd got wind of him being the sole survivor. Pride puffed out her chest. She was proud to have Charlie as her partner. She wished her well again for what lay ahead of the young DC and told her to call her after she'd left the exam.

I hope she doesn't flunk it after not sleeping all night. What a committed copper she is.

Roberts was the first to join her in the incident room.

"Hello, sir. How's it going?"

"Fine. Glad to have you back. I'll leave you to it." He turned and walked towards the door. "Sorry, how rude of me. How's Georgie?"

"I called the hospital first thing. They said she was a lot chirpier than she has been. AJ left at the same time as I did to be with her."

"You have a good man on your hands there, Katy. Be kind to him."

Katy frowned. "Meaning what?"

"Meaning don't go taking him for granted, either now or in the future."

"Excuse me? Since when does showing up at work give you the right to give me advice on my personal relationship? May I remind you of your position, sir? Divorced and living on microwave meals for one."

"Nasty retort. I didn't mean anything by my comment, only warning you what could happen in the future if you take your eye off the ball."

"I see. I'm glad we cleared that up," Katy snapped back. She stormed into her office and slammed the door hard enough for it to rattle in the doorframe for a few seconds after impact. *Jesus, what a frigging nerve. As if I haven't got enough shit to deal with right now. How dare he!*

She sat at her desk and sorted through the letters Roberts had placed into different piles. He couldn't even do that right. All the piles were jumbled up, only adding to her foul mood.

Karen knocked on the door with a cup of coffee ten minutes later. "Good to have you back, boss. Anything I can do to help?"

"Thanks for the coffee. No, I'll be out in a sec, after I've put these in the right places. Is everyone here?"

"Yes, all present and correct, except for Charlie. I hope things go well for her today."

"Me, too. She was at the hospital all night, guarding another victim. I'll tell you all about it in a few moments."

"No. That's dreadful. Poor Charlie. I'll leave you to it."

Katy smiled and put her head down once more. The phone rang, disturbing her when she was halfway through her task. "DI Katy Foster, how can I help?"

"I think I've been put through to the right person. This is Reverend Davison from St Bart's Church on Croft Road."

Katy's interest piqued at the name of the road. "I see. What can I do for you, Reverend?"

"I don't know how to say this but I think the man you're after is sitting in my church."

Katy shot out of her chair. "What? Oh heck, right. I'm on my way.

Do not approach him. Can you lock yourself in a room until I get there?"

"Yes. I'll do that. Please hurry."

"I'll be there within twenty minutes, I promise you." Katy ended the call. She pulled on her jacket en route and tore out of her office, firing off orders as she walked. "Let's go, Patrick, you're with me. He's at St Bart's Church on Croft Road. Karen, I need you to arrange for an ART to join us at the location. Graham, get that road blocked off, let's try and preserve as many lives as possible."

Katy barged through the outer door and down the stairs, two at a time, Patrick close behind her.

She stopped briefly at reception and filled the desk sergeant in while he signed out a Taser. "If your guys show up, I need them to be aware they could be in imminent danger, Mick. I don't want any hero-ics, you hear me?"

"Leave it with me, ma'am. Good luck."

The station's car park was a hive of activity. Katy headed towards her car, her heart racing, and pressed the key fob. Once inside, she fired up the engine and instructed Patrick to input the information into the satnav, a little unclear of the exact location they were aiming for.

"Right, yes, I think I know it now. Jesus, let's hope he's still there by the time we get there."

"Twenty minutes is an eternity for a man on the run, boss."

"Yep, I'm aware of that. We've got the Taser, get the pepper spray out of the glove compartment, will you? We might as well go the whole hog."

"I hope we don't need them and the ART will be on hand to take over."

"Yep, me, too."

Katy fell quiet and channelled all her attention into nipping in and out of the traffic, her siren emitting a stark warning not to toy with her.

They reached the location, only to find the road blocked by a patrol squad. Patrick and Katy leapt out of the car. A uniformed officer raised his hand to prevent them getting any closer to the church.

"Glad to see you're doing your job properly. I'm DI Katy Foster, SIO on this investigation."

"Sorry, ma'am, I should have recognised you."

Katy waved his excuse away. "The ART, are they here yet?"

"Not that I know of, ma'am. Want me to get on the radio to the other cars dotted around?"

"Yes, do that."

The answer was negative. *Damn, I can't wait for them, I need to get in there. Now.*

"Patrick, you and I are going in. Are you up for this?"

"You really have to ask me that, boss?"

"Not before we get geared up properly. In the boot you'll find a couple of stab vests. Some protection is better than nothing at all, right?"

Patrick scooted around the car and opened the boot. He returned wearing one of the vests and held out the other for her. "Tight fit, but as you say, it's better than nothing."

Katy slipped hers on and then pulled her jacket over the top again. "I feel safer already. Come on."

They walked along the pavement. Katy scanned the area for possible places where they could take cover at a moment's notice, should the need arise. The street was unnervingly quiet. A few curtains twitched now and again but, in the main, residents remained tucked safely behind their front doors.

Outside the church, Katy turned to Patrick and said, "Are you sure about this?"

He handed her the Taser and held up the pepper spray. "We've got this."

She wished she had his confidence. She inched towards the entrance and strained her ear to listen. Nothing but silence greeted her. *Is he still here? What if he's out here, hiding, spying on us, waiting to take a shot?*

Katy double-checked her surroundings and then gave Patrick the thumbs-up—they were going in.

She turned to enter the church, but something caught her eye at the end of the road. The ART had arrived, and now she was in two minds whether to go ahead with her planned entry or not. She shook her head and ordered Patrick to retreat.

"I can't do it. Our jobs could be on the line. I won't do it to you, mate."

He nodded his understanding, and the pair of them ran up the road to join their armed colleagues.

The commanding officer cocked an eyebrow at her. "You weren't about to do anything foolish then, were you, Inspector Foster?"

"Nearly. You took your time getting here."

"Less of the cheek and tell me what we've got. The intel we received was a tad scant to say the least."

"I take it you're aware of the shootings that have happened in the area over the past three days?"

"Very. Are you telling me the shooter is inside?"

"Possibly. The priest rang me around thirty minutes ago to inform me Boyd had shown up at the church. I told him to lock himself in a room. He swore he would stay put."

"You did right. Give me two minutes to plan the attack, and we'll see what we can do. I don't feel inclined to give this guy the opportunity to hand himself in. Am I wrong to think that?"

"I agree, although killing him outright isn't the answer either."

"I didn't say it was. Leave it to us, we'll bring your man down with enough force without harming him. That's the hopeful strategy anyway."

"Okay. Can we get a wriggle on?"

He shook his head and tutted. "Stand back."

She and Patrick took up their positions beside the team's vehicle.

Katy couldn't help feeling nervous about what lay ahead of everyone concerned. "What if he intends to go down fighting?"

Patrick shrugged. "There's no telling what's going to happen, boss."

Katy watched four armed policemen approach the church. She closed her eyes as they disappeared through the front door. They sprang open again when shots were fired.

"Shit! Not what I wanted."

The commanding officer demanded to know what was going on via the comms unit. Word came back that all was good and that the gunman had been apprehended. Moments later, the four officers and James Boyd emerged from the church.

Katy had a niggling doubt about the way things had gone down, it was too smooth for her liking. She kept a close eye on Boyd. He appeared to be mumbling. In the end, her fears proved to be unfounded. He was loaded into the back of the vehicle, accompanied by the rest of the team.

"We'll drop him off at the station for you. My guys have searched him and found no other weapons on his person," the commanding officer said.

"Great news. Thanks for your assistance today."

"It was our pleasure."

"All right if we go and check on the priest?"

"Yep, you're clear to do that."

Katy smiled her thanks and set off with Patrick.

"They worked smartly and efficiently," Patrick noted.

"They sure did."

Katy stepped into the church and called out, "Reverend Davison, are you here?"

A door creaked open behind the altar, and a pale old man wearing a dog collar and grey suit appeared. "I heard the shots. Please, tell me no one was hurt."

"They weren't, and it's all down to you. I can't thank you enough for getting in touch when you did. Do you have time for a brief chat?"

He gestured for them to take a seat on the front pew and let out a long sigh. "I'm so pleased I could help."

"Do you know James Boyd? Is he a parishioner?"

"He's been in here a few times in the past week. His confessions have rankled me. As you know, I'm not at liberty to tell the police what the general public confide during a confession, but I think the church will make an exception to that rule in this case, considering what he's done. He's not well, and no, that's not me trying to make excuses for the confused man."

"How do you know?"

"There were always two of them in the confessional, never just one man."

"Split personality?"

"I believe so, yes. The other voice came out occasionally when he was stressed. It scared me at times, but I could do little about it."

"It must have put you in an awkward position, sir, I'm sorry about that."

"Don't be. All is well now. Will you take his mental state into consideration whilst questioning him?"

"Yes, I'll ensure the interview takes place with an appropriate representative by his side. Perhaps you can divulge why he killed those people?"

"His marriage collapsed, that sent him over the edge."

"I suspected that might be the case. Okay, thank you for your time. Are you sure you're going to be all right?"

"Yes. I'll be fine. Thank you for showing up and dealing with the problem so promptly. I guess we can all sleep well in our beds tonight knowing that he'll be off the streets."

She held up her crossed fingers. "Take care, sir."

Katy and Patrick left the church and drove back to the station. First on the agenda, Katy visited Roberts to break the news. He was delighted and relieved that everything had gone well, although a little put out that he hadn't been involved in the final shootout.

Next step was to arrange for a psychiatrist to give them a brief evaluation before the suspect could be interviewed. In the interim, the news wasn't good. Boyd had melted down in his cell. He was found lying on the floor, a gaping wound to his head. He'd regained consciousness and kept saying over and over, "It wasn't his fault. He needed to rid himself of the voices."

Charlie dropped by the station after her exam.

Katy bought her a coffee and told her to take a seat. "Jesus, you look rough."

"No sleep has that effect on people," Charlie replied, clearly grateful for the caffeine fix. "I think it went well, though."

"Glad to hear it. Any idea when the results should be back?"

"A couple of weeks. Enough about me, how are things around here?"

"Oops...we've got him. Or should I say we had him." Katy raised a hand to prevent Charlie's interruption. "He's on his way to the hospital after smacking his head against the wall. He's not a well person. I can't see us getting the conviction we're after on this one."

"Ugh...not good. On the bright side, he'll be off the streets and London will be safe again."

Katy raised an eyebrow. "You reckon? I need to ring my hubby now. Get my own life back on track." She took her cup through to the office, leaving the rest of the team to celebrate the arrest and Charlie's good news.

EPILOGUE

A week later, and the case had been wrapped up and filed away as closed. Life was a little more settled for Katy now that Georgie was out of the woods and had been transferred to the children's ward, the next step before they allowed her to go home at the end of the week. AJ had been astounding. His strength and understanding floored her at times. She was so lucky to have him by her side.

He was spending less time at the hospital now at madam's request. Georgie had insisted her recovery would depend on the hours of play she could fit in with the nurses and the other children on the ward. Who were they to argue with her? This had allowed AJ to concentrate more of his efforts on getting his business off the ground. It was a few days after Christmas, their first where they hadn't all been together to share the festivities at home, but neither of them were perturbed about that. As far as Katy was concerned, every day would need to be a celebration in their house after the trauma they had been forced to endure over the past week.

Katy had received the news that Ben Thompson was now on the mend. It had been touch and go there for a while, but the doctor had told her that he was one of the most determined patients he'd ever come across in his time as a doctor.

James Boyd was a different matter entirely. He was now a resident in Broadmoor high-security hospital and the CPS were still debating whether he would go through a trial or not. She knew his psych evaluation would be taken into consideration before that decision was made. Katy felt sorry for the man, sort of, it was hard not to. The psychiatrist had informed her that the man had been battling his inner demons from a young age. The main trigger had been after his mother had died and his father took over being the primary parent and caregiver. He'd abused James mentally and physically since the age of seven. That torment had defined his future.

Memories of that torment had lain dormant for years until his wife had done the dirty on him and asked for a divorce. His behaviour had spiralled out of control the second Camilla moved out of the marital home and the frustration of not getting the promotion had driven him to kill.

Katy had no intention of heaping that blame on Camilla, who was now out of hospital and seeking psychiatric help of her own. After speaking with her a few days before, Katy knew the woman's resolve was strong enough to guide her on the right path to rebuilding her life in the near future; maybe after she'd laid Rufus to rest now his body had been released.

Life could be so complicated at times, proving only those willing to adapt would survive. Katy was one of those people, and so was her daughter, Georgie.

THE END

*T*hank you for reading my work, if you can find it in your heart to leave a review that would be amazing. There will be more for Katy and Charlie in March when Taste of Fury is published, until then, why don't you read another of my gripping thriller series? Here's the link to the first book in the DI Sara Ramsey series, **No Right To Kill**

KEEP IN TOUCH WITH M A COMLEY

Pick up a FREE novella by signing up to my newsletter today.
https://BookHip.com/WBRTGW

BookBub
www.bookbub.com/authors/m-a-comley

Blog
http://melcomley.blogspot.com

Join my special Facebook group to take part in monthly giveaways.

Readers' Group

Made in the USA
Las Vegas, NV
30 January 2021